Journal

Robert Thompson

Published by Sandwich Press, 2021.

JOURNAL

First edition. April 28, 2021.

ISBN: 979-8201129941

Written by Robert Thompson.

Table of Contents

To my family, my amigo and mentor Mark, my friends, and all of you who continually help me remember to dream.

William

I'm 10 years old, happily molded into an oversized beanbag chair in a warm, dimly lit room. The walls are sheathed with rough-cut cedar panels, and the entire space is artfully littered with toys and other small treasures. Sturdy shelves are stacked high with board games, books, puzzles, jars of jewel-bright marbles, and most of the other basic suburban childhood essentials. A row of model airplanes occupies a position of honor on the most prominent shelf, bookended by matching red Lava Lamps, which give the room its warm glow. It's a bit busy, but it has a very comfortable, cozy, 70s ambiance, complete with the Bugs Bunny show playing on a small black and white TV. It's the episode where Bugs is conducting the orchestra and an opera singer. My older brother and sister are there, but none of us are speaking. I know that we just finished a game of Parcheesi, because the game board is sitting on a low table next to me with the colored pawns crowding their home circles. In the back of my mind I know this isn't the house we live in, but I also know intuitively that this is "our" playroom. We're starting to put the game pieces away, but still nobody speaks, because we don't need to; conversation isn't necessary to the scene.

As I take in my surroundings, my focus becomes more clear, the room more familiar. I realize I've been in this playroom many times, and I remember that it's always the same – then I see the new door. It's always there, but each time it surprises me, because it always feels like a new discovery. I know this door leads to somewhere new, and that I want to go there, but it's always locked. I'm buzzing with nervous excitement because I sense that this time, something is different, so I stand up and shuffle across the thick carpeting to the new door. I twist the glass doorknob, push the door open, and walk into a new room. It's dazzlingly bright; inviting and pleasant, but very different from our playroom; like a seaside cottage sitting room that you reserve for more thoughtful days. The air shivers as a warm breeze stirs the sheer window dressings, and yellow sunlight streams in from large windows on three arcing walls that look out onto a sweeping ocean view. My eyes are drawn across the sprawling fields, to the busy village and harbor below the hill I'm looking down from. On the rim of the horizon I can just make out the silhouette of an old-fashioned sailing ship haloed by the sun, which overlays the entire panoramic vista with a glittering, golden blanket. There's a feeling in the room that I can't identify. I'm not sure how to define it, except to say that it feels right. A small writing table stands by the center window with an old, leather-bound book waiting patiently on it. It has the look of an artifact that has been in its place for a long, long, time – old, but not worn. As I approach it, a puff of wind ruffles the pages and leaves it open to a page with one hand-written word on it: William. Other than that, it's just a clean, bright white page. I flip to the next couple pages in the book and they're all blank.

If I had to put a word to the feeling of the room I would call it "curious," although I'm not sure if I'm curious about the room, or the room is curious about me. Could be either, but I think it's both – I think it wants me to be there. Turning away from the book I look around the room to find that there is nothing else of interest, not even a chair. It seems that the purpose of the room is to give place to the book. I notice that the door I came through has closed behind me. I reach for the doorknob, and everything fades to white.

. . .

"William?"

Now I'm awake in bed staring at the ceiling, just lucid enough to ponder on the thought that I'm 60 years old, and I've been having this same dream as long as I can remember. It's always the same, always ending right when I reach for the doorknob...except this time; all of a sudden, I'm allowed into the room. Why now – and why did I just think of myself as being *allowed* into the room?

Even in my groggy state it seems a little anti-climactic to have waited so many years for such a brief glimpse, but the bed is warm and I'm still in that perfect comfort a person only feels when they wake up before their alarm. I figure that gives me the right to sink back into my pillow and ruminate on my dream; however, a few minutes of thought is all it takes to be fully awake and know that I'm not drifting back into it. My clock has finally caught up with me, and I've never been successful at getting back to sleep to finish an interrupted dream anyway, so it's time to admit to myself that it really is time to get ready for work. Quietly dragging myself out of bed, I head into the bathroom with one small thought hanging on – who the hell is William?

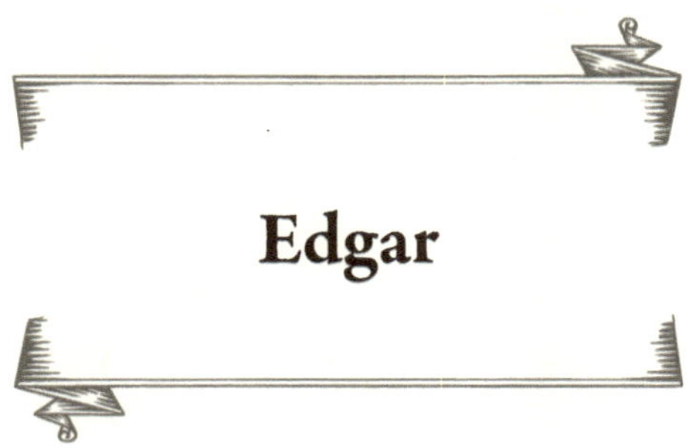

Edgar

Having a recurring dream for most of your remembered life, and then having it amend itself to reveal a book can tend to make you think of books, which is what I did all day today at work. I'm a graphic designer at an advertising agency, so I work closely with writers, and over the years I've come to respect their talents – and I've watched them and learned from them. Today I thought I'd be a little more observant and try to think about my dream from a writer's perspective, because, you know, books.

It gets me thinking about when books first took hold of me. I had just finished reading Patrick O'Brian's 20-volume series about a Napoleonic War-era British naval captain and his surgeon/spymaster companion. I enjoyed his stories so very much that when I reached the end of the series, I thought it would be impossible to ever love another book. I even read some of his other novels before I could let go. Eventually, though, I trusted another author with my fragile hope, and was rewarded for making the leap. Since then books have become my silent friends. Some I definitely get along with better than others, and some I can't stand to be away from for very long. Add the bonus of having middle-aged memory and I can even revisit them (more than once) and enjoy each reunion just as much as the first go.

I even toy with the idea of taking up writing, because anyone who loves to read should be able to write, right? After all, writing is only taking 26 letters and rearranging them in different combinations, isn't it? I suppose wanting to write springs from being a slightly frustrated artist. Make no mistake, I love to draw and paint, and I make my living doing just that. At one point in my life though, I became dispirited that it took so much time to create my work, which led me to explore photography as a way to capture images quickly – something my brushes didn't allow. It satisfied me for a time, but felt much the same, eventually leading me to the truth I had been trying so long to define. I had always held myself to a single, static image that was limited to my imagination, relatively disconnected from the imagination of anyone viewing my work. Words! They were the answer. The words in my silent friends' pages allow me to see every scene with my own eyes, and they do that for others as well, leaving our individual imaginations with absolute control.

After a day of shooting sideways glances at my wordsmith friends, I had received little more than a couple of "what are you looking at?" stares and reciprocal glances. Right before the 5 o'clock bell, Mark, my good friend and our staff's fearless leader, noticed my behavior and walked up to me.

He flashed a fake gang sign and said, "What's up Fop?" Mark is also the self-appointed nickname-giver for the agency staff. Thirty years working together, and I still don't know what mine means.

"Uh, nothing, just thinking."

"About...?"

"Never mind. You'll think I'm being goofy."

He smiled and raised both eyebrows in an unmistakable, that-ship-has-sailed expression.

"Okay, I was just thinking about a dream I had," I said.

"Is that why you keep staring at people?" he asked.

"Ah, you noticed that, did you?"

He chuckled. "Kinda hard not to."

"And here I thought I was being covert about it."

"No, I think pretty much everyone thinks you're casing their spaces for office supplies."

"Okay, it's about a dream I had, or a series of dreams really." I said hesitantly.

"About us?"

"No, they don't have anything to do with the agency," I said, before launching into a condensed version of the past dreams, and the recent, different one. Mark is one of my best friends, and is the first person I felt comfortable discussing it with outside my family, not because I didn't think he'd laugh at me, but because he pretty much laughs at me all the time, so I'm used to it. He's one of the few special people who can laugh at a person, but make it feel like he's laughing with them.

So after I accepted his witty and comedic barbs, he asked if I had any idea what it was leading to, and I had to say no.

"That's why I've been walking around today looking for clues, and by the way, I was only watching you writers, you know, for clues about why the book suddenly appeared," I said. "It didn't feel random, so I thought it was some kind of message."

"I guess I see the logic. You know, books are pretty wide-ranging as iconic symbols," he said. "It could mean almost anything. Maybe the book was just the first clue."

"Probably." I shrugged.

"If it is, I'm a little curious why it came to you as a book and not something more, you know, artsy," he said. "Because you're not really a writer."

"Hey, I write headlines sometimes!" My lack of conviction may have shown. "I get what you mean, though."

"Right! Well, let me know how it goes," he said, walking away. "And remember, if you can't write, call."

"Oh, and stop looking at people – it's weird," he adds as a parting shot.

Our brief conversation and my observations didn't lead me to any revelations about why, after decades of unvarying dreams, a book was suddenly important enough to be added to the storyline.

From the time I arrived at the office to the time I left, there was only one moment that brought me to a stop – when one of my cohorts who was carrying some boxes, said, "Would you please open the door again?" It wouldn't have garnered a second thought, but for the fact that I hadn't opened it up before that; it had to be a coincidence...

Seven and a half billable hours of confab and design wizardry later, with no new wisdom, I was ready to go home and don my artist uniform – which is pretty much the same thing I wore to work, but with comfy old-man slippers.

Home is where I do art for myself. My medium of choice is watercolor, which is a bit masochistic because watercolors have a will of their own – like a stubborn horse that wants to be back in the barn, or a herd of cats – pick your metaphor. I know this, because my wife is a horse person (not judging). I do however love what happens on paper when that watercolor horse is on its way back to the barn, or the paper in this scenario. The pigment, which is really a suspension of colored particles in water, drifts around until it settles in minute crevices in the heavily-textured paper, and follows the boundaries of the water in the area I'm working, sometimes leaving delicate capillaries traced around the edges. From the moment I touch the tip of the brush to the surface of the water on the sheet of paper, it starts deciding where it wants to go. Billowing out, bright clouds swirl and flow as millions of tiny colored grains whirl and glitter like shoals of fish in sunlit shallows. Sound cool? It is, and sometimes the surprise of what it does is the best part, so I climb into the saddle and try to ride along with the pigment's free will. A couple hours of painting a night is about all I can do without rudely transforming it from being something I want to do, to something I have to do, so after the ritual cleaning of the brushes it's time to put them down, and pick up a book.

I'm holding out hope for a return visit to the new room, so there's been more than a little anticipation building inside me all day. The more the minutes tick off, the closer I get to the same conditions that brought my new vision; that is, in bed, engaged in full REM sleep. The anticipation is probably a result of binge-watching too much TV, and becoming conditioned to believe that all conflict is resolved quickly (as it should be), right before the closing credits. In this case, that point of resolution seems to belong shortly after bedtime, so I have high hopes that I'm going to nod off and get some answers tonight, or at least one more.

Like most people, I use an alarm to mark the time that I get up in the morning, but the time I go to sleep is solely determined by what's unfolding in the book I happen to be reading each night at bedtime. You know what I mean – you have to finish the chapter, or at least the passage with the hero in peril, or else you'll abandon them to torment and danger until you can pick up your book again. So, now that Bilbo has narrowly escaped disaster again, I feel I am able to set my book down on the nightstand. He is safe and will remain so until I choose to insert myself back into his life. Although, kooky as it may be, in those moments between waking and dreaming I sometimes wonder if the characters in books are actually alive, and their existence is like a game of freeze-tag – that closing their book locks them in place, leaving them conscious but frozen in limbo, staring and waiting for their book to be opened so they can carry on with their story. Maybe that's why I don't like to leave them in a moment of peril. Okay, sometimes I do leave them there on purpose when I'm feeling cheesed-off. Weird I know, but I did grow up in the 60s.

At any rate, with my book safely at rest on the nightstand, I feel my eyelids getting heavy and my thoughts wandering. My thoughts tend to wander even in my waking hours, so it's no surprise that they started meandering away from the book

I was trying to urge them towards. In fact, they were ambling towards a barn, in the form of a watercolor-rendered horse. My mind did manage to hold on to a smidgen of my purpose – finding some answers – so I figured I should follow the horse. It was a very fluid dream, and the horse was easy to follow, since it was leaving multi-colored hoof prints wherever it walked. We were both immersed in the warm, clear brush water, and the pathway was alive with flowing color that was stirred by our steps before settling back into the ground, which in this case, was the watercolor paper. Even the trees swayed and bled color off into the water like lazy, drifting smoke. The horse showed an air of determination and picked up its pace as a falling crimson cloud settled in the distance to become his barn. A flock of small black birds sailed through the water overhead and followed us – they wanted answers too...

· · ·

Finally we reached the brightly colored barn and the horse stopped and began to graze in the impossibly green grass. It ignored me for a moment, and raised its beautiful head, tossing its flowing mane. He looked over at me in that way that a proud stallion does, at full attention, and posing in just the right way to appear regal and just a little haughty. His reddish-brown chestnut color glistened in the bright sunlight. Its eyes seemed to pierce my deepest thoughts but it remained silent as a book, waiting for me to turn the first page.

After a time I said, "I wish you could speak. I was hoping to find someone who could tell me about William."

The horse just stood there awhile, considering me. Then it took one step closer to me and said furtively, "Who the hell is William?"

Startled, I managed to reply, "Uh, I gather it's not you?"

"No, people call me Edgar Allen Pony," he said with a slightly imperious tone.

"Wait, what?" I said. "But, if you're not William, why did you lead me here?"

"Lead you here?" he said, "I did not lead you here, you followed me. Why did you do that, anyway?"

"Because I came here to find out about the book, and who William is."

The horse studied me again and said, "Okay, I'll bite, what book?"

"The book in my dream..."

"In this dream?" he asked.

"No, in my other dream."

"Really," he said, "how am I supposed to know about a book in your other dream?"

"I don't know," I said, "none of this is making any sense."

"But you thought asking a horse about a book would? You know horses can't read, right?"

"This is all so confusing," I said.

He paused thoughtfully and asked, "Want some hay?"

"No, thanks, Edgar. I'm obviously in the wrong place."

"Well, do let me know if you find William," he said.

"Thanks," I said, "I better go. I need to find some answers"

"That you do," he replied with genuine concern.

I thank Edgar for his kindness, push off the ground and rise through the water, passing through the flowing trees, emerging into an aqueous sky that sparkles and glows.

As I fly out of view, one of the curious birds lands on a railing next to Edgar and says, "Who was that?"

With a knowing look, Edgar says, "Some guy looking for William."

. . .

I lie there with sleep in my eyes thinking – this isn't going to be easy.

Journal

Days pass, and I'm not doing any better at dropping back into the dream to find out who William is. I have no family member, friend or acquaintance named William who would be familiar enough to me to bring sense to this message. I have had other dreams, most of them just as confusing and kooky as meeting Edgar, but none even hinting at new doors, William, or the book. Edgar seems to know more than he lets on, which seems unusual, at least with the few other horses I've met. When I stop to think about it, I realize my dreams prior to being shown the book were fairly few and far-between, but regular enough that I feel like they are a message, and not just the monotonous repetition of a boring dreamer. There must be a reason why I had to wait so long; and the addition of the book must be a clue that I have to work out myself. If that is the case, then I have some other answers to find before the bigger ones can be revealed, and the incentive to take the time to do it.

Now instead of a couple questions I have about a thousand, the first of which is – what do I need to do to find answers? My first thought with any task in my life is to make copious notes and over-plan, so I'm thinking it is Journal Time. I kept regular journals for years when I was younger, but got busy with life and eventually fell out of the practice. Back then I really enjoyed organizing my thoughts on paper, and I still pull out my old journals from time to time to reflect on who I was and who I've become. Thinking about starting up again feels good, and I have a strong impression that the timing is right. One of my favorite diversions is reading through an old journal and finding that events that used to intimidate me now seem simple, almost effortless. It's a lesson my journals taught me long ago, that struggles strengthen us, and if we don't recognize our own growth, it's only because our trials increase along with our ability to deal with them. Looking back has helped me recognize the strengths I possessed as a younger man – stronger faith, more compassion and selflessness, and much more innocence.

It's been so long since I quit keeping a journal that I feel pretty strongly about rereading them, and putting some honest effort into filling in the major events I neglected to record. After a couple weeks of going through my old entries, I've come to a couple conclusions. First, I guess I already was a writer, albeit not a very good one. Second, and more importantly, I was writing about important things. I'm not sure why this surprises me, because I was writing about the highs and lows of my life, but it still touches me deeply, in ways I was not expecting. I am finding it cathartic to see this young man with his whole life ahead of him, writing about his love for his young bride and his growing family. Strangely, I hardly recognize myself in many of my old entries. They almost seem to have been written by different person. Another realization hits me hard – the cost of the missing pages. Reading a passage about the birth of one of our children, and then turning the page to see I skipped making journal entries for the next two weeks makes me ache for the missing memories of what I did with all that time. Being 60 makes it all the more acute. Knowing that it was likely a trial or challenge that took my attention away from writing makes me feel like an amnesiac racked with the loss of their personal identity. How much different would I be if I remembered who I was on those days? Is that why we see our life flash before our eyes when we die? I had always been pessimistic about that concept, thinking all I would see is every mistake and bad decision I had made – all the regrets. Now I think it's also to remind us of all the good things that happened, and the things we did right, so we can relive all the lost days, and realize who we are as a whole, before we step into the next adventure after our life.

I had been worried that starting up my journal again might be a distraction, but it seems like the best way to keep this whole thing together in a way that makes sense – and, I can't stand the thought of losing any more days – any more of my self. There is also something else below the surface. I'm not sure what it is, but I think I'm getting close to it.

Kate

Weeks later I've made some progress at getting caught up on my journal, but there are still years to make up. Oh my, how the time has flown – not all because we've been having fun. Still, many good things have happened, and the hard parts have brought light and wisdom along with them, at least when I was paying attention. Our family has wrestled with everyday life like most people do. We've lost family members and friends, as well as some people who we did not know well, but still touched our lives. Some of my old entries brought back memories that felt like opening up old wounds, yet with the years that have passed, they don't hurt as much – they just make me more reflective and appreciative of what I had, and have. Some of these more distant connections still grip me deep inside, in a way that is difficult to express. One entry crystallized that thought for me. It had to do with one of my entries I was reading at bedtime, about a particular day at work.

Journal entry - August 16, 2010

One of the things they don't tell you in graphic design school is that lots of people will ask you to create things for them like birthday cards, graduation announcements and wedding invitations for their loved ones. And then there are the funeral programs. Funeral programs have always been hard for me. It is an honor to share life events with people, and help people through good times and bad, but there is a process I go through, as I work on them alone. Even if I'm not close to the person who passed, what I feel when I learn about them links me to them in ways that are not obvious to others, and I've felt a lot of grief as I've created them. I've lost track of how many I've put together over the years, and the one I started today was a hard one. If I was a writer I could find words to explain it, but I'm not, and it may not matter anyway, because I know it will never fade from my mind.

Rereading this entry, and other rekindled memories prompts me to switch out the book on my nightstand. My journal will now take over the place of honor next to the bed. Since I began my manhunt for William, it's caught my attention more than the idea of finishing *The Hobbit* one more time – it feels a little more pressing, because I know Bilbo will wind up safely back at Bag End in the end, even if I don't walk along beside him. So after today's entry, I put down my journal and turn off the light, then close my eyes knowing he'll probably be fine.

. . .

I'm stunned to find myself in the bright room again. The scene is the same as before – light is streaming in, bringing with it a fresh, pleasant breeze. Wasting no time, I walk straight to the table with my fingers crossed, prepared to find more clues about William. Looking down at the book I see one word written on the open page - Kate.

What?

If I was astonished before, it was nothing to what I am now. I was picturing seeing William where he was supposed to be, with his life story written out in beautiful script flowing across the page, and now - Kate?

I'm standing there trying to work through my confusion, looking out the bay windows, indifferent to the ship I saw the last time I was here, still slowly navigating up the channel towards the harbor, trying to find its way in, just like me.

Either a little or a lot of time passes and I have the feeling that this is all I'm getting, so I turn and reach for the doorknob and walk back into the playroom – except it's not the playroom, it's my office – with me, sitting at my computer, focused on my screen. So now I'm astonished again. I see myself sitting there looking at the images on the big flat-panel monitor. My head is resting on my hands, and my shoulders are shaking. I walk around to the side and notice that I'm crying – no, I'm flat-out bawling my eyes out. The photos on the screen explain why, and it all comes flooding back.

Oh...Kate.

The project I have up on my computer is a funeral program I was creating a few years ago for a young lady named Kate. She was a beautiful, bright-eyed 16-year-old whom I never even met, but still felt an ache about, knowing how her life was cut short so unfairly. She was killed in a plane crash in southwest Alaska, along with her mother and a number of others, including a prominent public figure. Now both of my selves are crying our eyes out. Of the many funeral programs I've been asked to do for friends and relatives, Kate's affected me the most profoundly.

I remember that Kate's mother worked for one of our clients, so, shortly after the crash we were contacted by a representative from her office, and we were given photographs of Kate and the pilot, whose program I also did. Along with the photographs, there were other personal items – some artwork Kate had done, a poem she had penned titled "One Perfect Rose," and some written notes from their families lovingly illustrating who they were, what they loved – what they dreamed of and accomplished. Aside from the small pile of photos and notes on my desk, I knew nothing about Kate, and of the pilot, nothing but his stellar reputation in the Alaska aviation community. There was enough however to make a small but powerful connection to Kate – not a personal connection, but still an overwhelming sense of the life force in her that wanted to do and be so much more than she was given time for. Many people never realize how vast their full potential is, but here was a soul that seemed to have a vision of what could be; not specific as to where she would go, who she would meet, or what she would ultimately do in her life, but full of the promise of knowing it would be a grand adventure. She would walk around walls or climb over them without hesitation. But maybe Kate didn't need to – maybe her soul was pure enough that she didn't have to take that test.

. . .

I cover my head with my pillow and think, "Not what I was expecting."

I was thinking (and hoping) that my search was going to be like *Goonies* or some other fun, rollicking adventure puzzle where I mysteriously receive cool, orderly clues; that if I thought enough about the next dream I wanted, my mind would take me there. Instead, this feels more like waking life, where you have "growth opportunities" that happen when you supposedly need them.

I really hate growth opportunities.

As much as I had wanted my dream to lead me to something new, this was much different than what I expected – but I have to think this is happening for a reason, because that's just me. Even before I ever thought about spiritual things, I always had a sense that there was some sort of intelligent order to life. It was fun to imagine that I was a sort of spiritual being having an earthly existence, and to believe in magical things and happy endings.

So if this is a growth opportunity, what is the lesson?

Every program I had created before Kate's had been difficult, because I had known the person who had passed, or members of their families, so why should Kate's affect me so much more dramatically? The answer to that question wasn't written on the page in the book, it wasn't on my computer screen – it was still beyond my reach. I suppose it brought back some of the painful memories in my own life, maybe things I was still hanging onto. In the back of my mind I knew there was something I was missing, or I would have felt peace.

There was just the despair and aching, and the universal question – why?

Journal entry - January 20, 2019

My dream last night left me spinning. I would think it was all random but for the fact that it's been weeks since I had a dream about the room. Maybe the fact that I had just read my old entry about Kate was why I had that specific dream. It would've been nice if it finished with a neat bowtie of a thought that helped me move forward. Instead, it leaves me tapping my head like Winnie the Pooh. I'm beginning to think that in addition to whatever grand epiphany is waiting for me, I'm also supposed to learn patience.

This is really not going to be easy.

True North

I know and appreciate the old adage that progress happens by taking "two steps forward, one step back," but this undertaking seems reversed. As much as I'm enjoying writing in my journal again, recording my perspective of our family's story, I'm always drawn back to my old journals. Remember when I said being in my 60s allows me to reread a book and enjoy it just as much as the first time? It seems it's true for my own scribbles as well. I find an anchor in revisiting the older parts of our story; like, it's easier to see where you're going when you know where you've been. I wouldn't liken it to clinging to the "glory days," it's more like what you feel when you're navigating the countryside with a map and compass. The outdoorsy geek in me knows that a sure way to keep a true course is to line up your compass and map with the direction you want to go and find a landmark on the path along that bearing. When you walk to the landmark and turn to look back, you can take a reciprocal bearing from your last landmark to see if it agrees with the heading that you just took, and if doesn't, you just shift your position left or right until the two bearings cancel each other out. Looking back to what my goals and dreams were when I was younger casts a bright light on where I am now. All my headings don't line up exactly, but then, we are allowed to change our minds about where we want to go.

Anyway, the steps back have helped me understand how I got here, and I trust them, because they've helped me see I'm moving forward – more or less on course.

My hope that I would see what I expected to see, when I expected to see it has been replaced with, yup, more questions. I have no idea what's coming next, but who really does?

Question for the universe: When the wind blows the pages of the book to my next clue, is that akin to the universe throwing caution to the wind? So far it kinda feels like it. With that thought in mind, I've taken to picking up one of my old journals, opening it to a random page, and reading whatever is there. I figure I'm trusting to the wisdom of the universe because that's the way my dreams seem to be coming.

So far, my random-page journal reading technique has been fruitful. Even with the days rolling past, I don't feel like I'm marching rigidly down a fixed timeline, I'm just ambling along, viewing glimpses of our lives, and it leaves me smiling, even when I turn to a page that is recalling a difficult time. I feel peace when I recall the ones that were resolved in the end. That conclusion stays with me throughout the day, right up to bedtime.

. . .

I'm back in the new room, but nothing has changed. I'm still staring at the Kate's page with no idea what I'm supposed to do. I can feel the sun coming through the window on my face. The end-of-day glory light is growing and draws me over to the far side of the room. The windows on that side frame the kind of scene that artists paint because they can't find worthy words to write about them. The prideful painter in me is now thinking, "I defy any writer to describe this with mere words," and it's clear to me why we have pens and paint brushes. The hues are a thousand shades of gold that pull me outside, so I'm now wandering through them under a blue sky so startling and pure in color that as an artist I can only describe it as straight-out-of-the-tube. My mind is also wandering, and pondering. I realize I'm not the only one there and look up to see two people a short distance away – a woman, and a young lady, walking down a lane that cuts across the field. It's a serene vision; it doesn't have a material feel; it's above earthly qualities – there is no darkness. I watch them walk and talk and laugh for some time, taking in this picture of joy and innocence, and the woman – I'm sure she's the girl's mother, says, "Let's go home, Kate," and all I feel is peace and resolution.

. . .

Journal entry – February 20, 2019

They're okay...I got to see Kate and her mom, and they're ok. Why did I get to see it? Who let that happen?

It's resolution. I get to bring the peace and resolution with me. Or am I leaving something else there? I don't know if I care which is happening – it just doesn't matter. I had to rush to my journal and put this down so I wouldn't forget the smallest detail of what I'm feeling and thinking now. The peace and simplicity of this knowledge has the same intensity and richness as the colors I saw in the field.

That it's real and true, I have no doubt, just as surely as I know the sun is shining on my face when my eyes are closed. There is too much purpose evident for it to be random, especially with my history of ridiculous and meaningless dream content. My compass is leading me. I'm not sure where yet, but I'm looking forward to my next landmark.

The Old Names

Today I flipped open one of my journals to an entry where I recorded the experience of finding a distant ancestor while I was working on my family history years ago. I was pretty seriously into genealogy when I was in my early 30s and spent a fair amount of time doing research, primarily at the National Archives in my hometown. It sounds like tedious work, but when you're sifting through pages of archival records, you can't help but appreciate the implications of the lists. Each name beautifully preserved with pen and ink in meticulous calligraphic script represents a life event of an individual who spent their years searching for the same happiness that we hope for today. Even people who are not relations speak to you when you see mother, father and children's names, elegantly penned – an important moment of a family captured. I experience an even more profound sense of fulfillment whenever I locate one of my ancestors.

I've always loved how some cultures speak collectively of their forebears as their Fathers and Mothers, as a respectful way to express the reverence they hold for the multitude that are their ancestors. It occurs to me that those titles are also literal in many instances, as in, more than one father. In my short 60 years, I have had four. My father that helped bring me into this world, and raised me to the age of 15, left me with a precious handful of truths that, in large part, shaped me. Even when he was at his lowest point in life he was still teaching me. I say precious because he's not here to give me any more. I could sum them up in a few phrases: be honest, do the right thing, do your best, and keep the tip of your fishing pole up. Our daughter is now older than he was when he died.

My stepfather was my dad's friend, and took it upon himself to try to fill in his shoes as best he could, and he did a very good job, without trying to replace him. He built on what my father had tried to teach me, in much the same manner. He taught me how to strive for perfection. He left me with more of the same values my father had, and more importantly, an increased appreciation for my dear mother, who I had previously failed to see through the eyes that he had for her. One of his nicknames for her was "Princess", ad she really was, and I didn't realize how little I knew her until it was too late.

My father-in-law was a tough and colorful man who exemplified the title of pioneer. Half German and half Alaska Native, he grew up in Bush Alaska. He taught me how to work, how to take care of my family, and to never, ever, give up. Now, like my other fathers, he's taught me how to say goodbye.

It's not a stretch for me to speak of these men as my fathers, with that same collective meaning, and the literal one as well. The biology doesn't matter, the mixing of lives does. Families are not accidents of genetics, they are built with purpose, or they do not fulfill the meaning of the word. Working to build a life with someone can create the dream that can't always be found.

My fourth father is the one I talk to in private.

Man I get preachy when I start cogitating on deep topics.

Steph

After a very hectic and frustrating week, Stephanie and I found ourselves needing a restorative Saturday afternoon road trip. Not a trip with a specific purpose, just one of those spur-of-the-moment "let's get out of town for the day" excursions that couples do. They usually involve grabbing phones, wallets, jackets, snacks, and of course, a camera because, Lord, we do take pictures of everything.

Our favorite short road trip is to hop on the Seward Highway and trundle along Turnagain Arm, named after another of Captain James Cook's failed attempts to find a Northwest Passage from the Pacific to the Atlantic Ocean in 1776. He was way off that time too and had to "turn again", as the short, treacherous body of water only extends about 40 miles into the border of the Chugach and Kenai mountains, and is scoured twice daily by ferocious 30-foot tides of churning, silty seawater. The Seward Highway follows the twists and turns of Turnagain Arm in a way that reveals the stunning scenery one frame at a time, each curve opening up a new perspective that changes its appearance by the minute.

Even a crummy-weather day has its own brand of beauty on that narrow ribbon of blacktop, and it always lives up to its designation as a National Scenic Byway, so it never fails to provide plenty of natural beauty to gush over.

As we drove, our conversation varied as much as the scenery and eventually turned to the topic of my dreams. We hadn't talked about it in a while, so in her no-nonsense way, Steph switched gears and said, "Find any new doors or rooms lately?"

"Not since the door that led to my office that day," I replied, having expected it to come up.

"The day you were doing the funeral programs?" she asked.

"Yeah, I've just been going over my old journals, reading the old ones, and trying to catch up and fill in holes where I wimped out on them."

"Any new names pop up?" she asked.

"So far just William, Edgar, and Kate. And Kate is the only one who is a real person I know of."

"Don't say that to Edgar," she replied.

"Edgar knows something, and he's not being very forthcoming," I said with a sour tone.

"He sounds like a smart horse!"

"Smart aleck is more like it."

"He just wants you to keep searching is all," she said.

"Are you gonna lay some sophisticated barnyard wisdom on me now?"

"It's just good horse sense."

"Ok, go ahead, let's have it," I said.

"How about – the ox is slow but the Earth is patient..."

"Isn't that from a low-budget Kung Fu movie?" I asked.

"High Road to China, that old Tom Selleck movie."

"Right...the Tibetan monk...did he explain what it meant?" I said.

"Something about patience I think."

"Patience? Me? Way to hit below the belt."

"I'm sure Edgar will come around," she said.

"Edgar is in the barnyard and he's there to stay. I should've just asked the birds that were following us," I replied.

"What birds?"

"Never mind, you know my dreams are all mindless meanderings."

"So...any new thoughts on William?" she asked.

"Nothing. I'm being led everywhere but back to William." I said. "He could be anyone. I haven't gotten one clue about who he is, but he was the first one, so that has to mean something, right?"

"Maybe you just have some other things to figure out first and William is the carrot on the stick." She said with a grin. "I'm sure it'll come to you, maybe in your next dream."

"Thanks for not thinking I'm a kook about all this."

"It seems like there's something else here, it seems too connected to not have a conclusion."

"That's what I keep saying, too." I replied, as we started making our back.

The tide was going out as we were getting back into town. City traffic is the surest of ways to lose one's concentration on an elusive thought, and sure enough, I drove the rest of the way home only managing to wonder what else there was.

That night I fell back on my habit of diving into old journals to search for further clues, and I found a newer-looking journal that I didn't recognize. I figured it must be the last one I had started, and I had just forgotten about that particular volume. I was partly right; I had forgotten about it, in fact, after opening it up to the first page, I hadn't even remembered starting it.

Right...Stephanie.

Years ago, my wife's sweet mother was having the struggle of her life. She was suffering the results of a combination of heart attacks and strokes that left her unable to move or speak, or even blink to communicate, even though she was completely present mentally. Steph was spending much of her time every day and most nights attending to her mom, and it took her away from us quite a bit. I had begun this separate journal to put down all the thoughts I was having about what she was doing, as a way for her to stay connected to us while she was spending so much time away.

I had the kids write some entries to her at the beginning, and I entered daily messages for her to read later, and kept it up for about a month. About then, another one of those lost days happened and I missed doing an entry, and then another, and another, until distraction totally pushed it from my mind. My last entry was 20 years ago, almost to the day. Here was one more of the "something else" things.

This feels like one of those mistakes of my life that will flash before my eyes before I die. It's definitely a big article of regret. I dropped what could have been a powerful bond between us because I, what, got busy? It should have been a storybook moment, and I missed it. Maybe this is just a second chance. The only thing to do is have our now-grown kids make a last entry and present it to her 20 years too late.

How to See

Journal entry – March 31, 2019

It came to me today I may be ignoring one of my primary tenets of becoming an artist.

Backing up though, I've been drawing since I was a kid, and painting since college. It never occurred to me to ask myself why. It's just always been a part of me, and it's been my livelihood. When people show appreciation for my work, they frequently tell me they can't even draw a stick man and my standard reply is, "Sure you can, you just have to learn how to see." Most don't get my meaning, so I usually end up explaining my belief that learning to draw is really learning how to see, much like learning music is all about learning to hear. We humans see and hear what we expect to, because that's how our brains are wired. The mind wants to neatly package the almost infinite details that our senses gather, and it does that by generalizing all of that information.

Here's how my theory works. When you look at a farm scene, your brain tells you, "Oh, look – a pretty farm." If you take the time to look more closely though, you see the elements that make up that pretty farm. You see the grass and the barn and the trees and the sky. Look closer at the barn and you'll see the light wrapping around it, shading and hiding details on the dark side and drawing your eye to the brighter colors and sharper detail on the other. Now, take the time to really pay attention to the walls, and you'll pick up the weathered textures; the rusty reds and the shaded hues that you first thought were black or gray, are revealed to be blues and purples, reds and greens, changing and blending as the subtle reflected light plays across the scuffed and uneven surface of the planks. You notice small shafts of sunlight peek through cracks and throw bright lines on the grass. Look closer, and you'll see what you're looking at more accurately, and by the same reasoning you'll also be able to tell if whatever you're drawing has been captured accurately.

So, I've been forgetting that life follows those same rules. I'm seeing what I expect, or want to see, because I want it to be easy to understand. I'm going to start looking for the subtleties from now on.

If I'm honest, I'll admit that I'm just repackaging truth my mother tried to teach me when I was little – "If you can't find it, go back and look harder." I've been going back...now I'm going to look harder. Maybe this also answers the "why do I paint" question – I paint, because I need to. Without it I am certain that I would find other means of expression and introspection. In fact, I already dole out my time to other activities that help me find my center. I frequently tell people that I'm just as happy with a hammer in my hand as I am with a paintbrush.

This fresh perspective has gotten me fired up to continue pressing forward, so I begin by going back to look harder – in my old journals. I know it seems literal, but I figured I'd start with literal and move on to figurative if that didn't pan out.

It didn't pan out.

I spent several days poring over old entries and didn't find any Easter eggs anywhere. I'm calling this day done and I'll pick it up again tomorrow with fresh eyes. I kiss Steph good night, reach over to turn out the light, hit the pillow with a finality that echoes my frustration, and drift off to sleep.

. . .

I'm drifting through warm water again, sinking downwards in a swirling cloud of cerulean blue pigment that glows where the light shines through. The little black birds are following me again, and I can see details forming as I get closer to the field of paper spread underneath me. I touch down lightly and head straight for the barnyard with my wingmen in tow, to find Edgar and press him for answers, or at least try to read between the lines of our prior conversation. Edgar is nowhere in sight, but the birds are flitting here and there, following me around the barnyard as I look for him. I walk around the barn, past a pond, over to a large field and back to the barn, where five of the birds are perched on a fence rail watching me.

I'm standing there, hands on my hips wondering where to look harder, when the middle bird says, "Dude, looking for something?"

Again, not what I expected, but I reply, "Uh, yes, I'm looking for Edgar."

"Edgar who?"

"Edgar Allen Pony, you know, the horse."

"You mean Buck the horse? A Morgan, about 15 hands?"

"Yeah, maybe. He told me his name was Edgar Allen Pony." I said, as three of the birds fall off the fence laughing.

The bird chuckles, "Yeah he was messing with you, his name is Buck. Actually what he said was, that's what people call him. People always feel the need to give animals new names."

"Okay, is Buck here then?" I asked

"Buck who?" he said, "Sorry man, just messing with you. No, he's not here, I'm not sure where he went."

"Okay, fine. What do people call you, then?"

"Mr. Tibbs" replied the bird with a wink to his remaining fence mate. "Just kidding, bud. My name is Bob."

"Of course it is," I said with a sigh.

"What do people call you?" he asked.

"Right now? Frustrated."

He paused, sizing me up. "Yeah, I remember you came here before, looking for William."

"Right, I did, and I can't help but notice that you said that like you know him," I said, looking hard at Bob in return.

"Oh, everyone here knows William."

"Then why didn't you say something last time?" I said through gritted teeth.

"Yeah, I don't know. What do you want to know about William for?" He asked, with a suspicious tone.

"Because I dreamed about his name, and I need to find out who he is and how I'm connected to him. I know I need to look closer at things I've seen to find the truth – that's why I came back!"

He studied me a moment longer. "Just hang in there, buddy, keep searching, it'll come."

Growing flustered, I said, "Seriously? That's all you have to say to me?"

He paused, and with solemn dignity, said, "The ox is slow, but the earth is patient."

I feel myself floating upwards again, which means I've missed my chance to smack Bob off the fence rail. I'm alone, high in the sky, breaking through the puffy clouds. I feel myself being swept away as if by a giant brush.

Actually, it is a giant brush. A big red one.

Whatever.

"What do you think, Bob?" says the second bird on the fence.

Bob pauses and says, "He's getting there."

"Right, the ox is slow. I think maybe he is too," replies the second bird.

. . .

Before my eyes are even open, the words are already on my lips – "I really hate birds."

Go ahead, Laugh

The famous French philosopher Voltaire once said that he thought God is a stand-up comedian playing to an audience that is too afraid to laugh. Am I supposed to take my bird dream as a hint that I need to have a better sense of humor about my life? Or, was that the universe giving me the bird?

I could easily accept learning the mysteries of life from a bird if I was receiving them from a wise, stately owl or something a little more impressive. Maybe you get the bird you deserve, figuratively speaking. I definitely have been given the bird I deserve at other times.

Separating the bird from the message, I guess I'm supposed to exercise my patience and be the ox – or am I the earth? Whichever I'm supposed to be, I'll try to apply a good sense of humor to it.

I love working in downtown Anchorage because it's adjacent to the Coastal Trail, a 26-mile, curvaceous bike path that snakes around the city's surrounding coastline. It's a great place to take a quiet stroll to clear my head and take in some natural goodness and beauty. There aren't too many places outside Alaska where you can go to see such an abundance of scenery and wildlife inside your city limits. It's a bit slow today so I'm taking some extra time to just chill and jot some things down in my current journal, with patience and a sense of humor, mind you.

I got comfortable on a bench overlooking Knik Arm and made a lengthy entry mapping out everything I could think of that I picked up so far from my dreams, my old journals, and the thoughts I've had about how it all ties together. Then I tried to read between the lines to figure out what I could have missed. I'm beginning to see more connections, and even though the messages have come in different ways, I sense that they are linked and will lead me to William somehow. As I sat there watching the tide slowly make its way in, a shadow passed over me, followed by the faint splat of something wet landing on my open pages.

"Nice Bob, good to see you too," I said, as I wiped the bird droppings off my last entry with dry leaves, gathered up my things, and headed back to the office.

I feel like I passed a test, since I didn't react to the dive-bombing bird by chucking rocks at it. There was no real damage done, and I even noticed that the flying poo landed squarely upon the passage I had just written about the ox and the earth, and having a sense of humor in the face of trials. Could Bob possibly be that subtle *and* accurate? All of a sudden I have a new respect for Bob the Bird.

After thinking about it, it actually seems like a pretty solid affirmation that my head is in the right place. I think I might even be starting to like Bob. He kind of reminds me of me. He certainly has left his mark on me, or, my journal. So much so that when I got back to the office, a coworker and friend, John, saw the smile on my face and said, "Did you have a good walk then?"

I said, "It was great except for one little thing."

"Well, shit happens." He replied, not knowing how right he was.

Speaking of words

Did I mention I like books? Well I do. Besides my love of good stories I have a deep-seated love of words, and a compulsive need to understand where they come from. One of my favorite obsessive behaviors is looking up the etymology of words online to see if there is a good backstory behind the root of a word – because words rock.

Today I was scrolling through social media, wondering where the term "meme" came from. I was just thinking about how many secrets of life were contained in the infinite number of memes floating around in the cloud instructing us all on the sure-fire ways to fix everything wrong in our lives, and figured with something so important and necessary to us, it must have a very weighty and grave origin.

I had always assumed it was a term created by a hip tech guru meaning "Me, me!" as in, "Look at me!" My need to know took over, and after a quick web search I discovered (thanks to *Science Friday*) that the term "meme" was in fact, coined by evolutionary biologist Richard Dawkins in his 1976 book, *The Selfish Gene*. Dawkins blended the Greek word "mimeme" meaning "to imitate," with the word "gene," to describe what he saw as a new replicator in the modern primeval soup which he believes is human culture. That is a deep bowl of soup.

As much as I like to project my persona as being above things as cheesy as memes, I do secretly appreciate one that is cleverly done. I'm sure it's the adman in me, knowing that the purest form of advertising is the infamous highway billboard, which is most effective using no more than seven words. Dr. Seuss, along with every good creative in the ad biz, knows that the ultimate challenge is to tell a story with a limited number of words.

One meme I stumbled onto today was an all-text message on a cartoony scroll background, listing six simple thoughts about faith, hope, and love. I particularly liked the first one, which said, "Once, all the people of a village decided to pray for rain. On the day of prayer, all the people gathered, but only one little boy came with an umbrella. That is faith."

Kids get it. They're still innocent enough not to doubt and question everything that comes to them. It makes them vulnerable, but their innocence allows them to live in a world of peace and joy that too many of us lose track of – like me for example.

Another of my old journal entries reminded me of a time I saw this play out in real life with stark plainness, when years ago, one of our kids suffered severe burns as a toddler, requiring him to be hospitalized. The day after the accident, he was already tired of being cooped up in his room, so I took him for a walk down the hallway, with his little arm and chest thickly bandaged, and an IV bottle hanging from a wheeled rack. He wasn't complaining – just walking along, smiling and saying hi to everyone he saw; no shred of doubt or worry in his mind. He wasn't questioning whether he would recover. It never even occurred to him that quitting was something to consider – quitting is a concept unknown to childhood innocence.

The older I get, the more I want to become as a little child. It's not an easy thing for an old guy who has piled on layers of armor to protect himself from what *might* happen – armor that also screens him from feeling hope, trust, and love.

Number two on the meme said, "When you throw babies into the air, they laugh because they know you will catch them. That is trust."

I think maybe I'll try a little harder to hope and trust – and laugh; and more importantly, to remember to be there for people when they are trusting that I'll catch them. Maybe if I can, I'll be able to shed a little of the armor and be more receptive to the quiet messages that will lead me to the end of this quest.

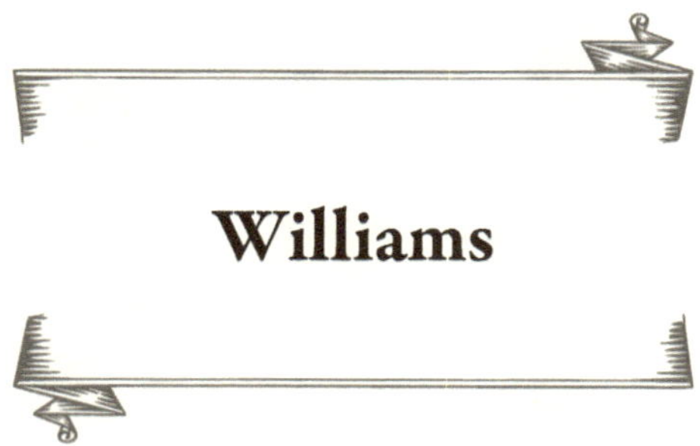

Williams

I've been practicing hope, trust, laughter, and patience a lot, and I think it's beginning to help. I've noticed a change in my attitude – and I think it's reshaping me in a fundamental way.

That being said, do you have any idea how many friggin' Williams there are in the world? Since the beginning of this quest I've begun to notice. It's very much like when you stub your toe, and for the next week discover every out-of-place object in your house by inadvertently kicking them, repeatedly, with that same swollen toe. Lately everywhere I go I've been bumping into William's name – on furniture store signs, law offices, historical figures, universities, princes – even a pretentious-looking Shih Tzu with a bejeweled collar, and not one of them has walked up and said hi to me. I was hoping for signs, but not literally. It's gotten so relentless that it's becoming a distraction.

It kind of reminds me of something. Oh right, me. It is almost impossible for me to hold things in. If I have a thought, it's pretty much coming out. I'm quite sure that when I was a kid, I was the one following my mother around saying, "Mom, Mom, Mom, Mom, Mom..." And now William is doing it to me.

Growth opportunity?

I think the universe is applying Bob the Bird's subtle manner to pressure me to bust a move. If the universe is as smart as everybody thinks, it should know that I'm busting moves left and right, as fast as I know how.

Right...patience.

I just wish I could get this whole learning patience thing over with quicker. I'll start tomorrow...

. . .

I'm sitting in the playroom again with my brother and sister, only this time I'm not rushing towards the new door. I've just been sitting and watching them for a long time because it occurred to me that the dream has always been about me getting through, alone. It also occurred to me that we go through things alone because in our heads we are alone, unless we let someone else in there. I sit there in my cozy oversized beanbag and my years-long dream always begins by me walking away from my siblings without a second thought. In all the times I've been here, I've been so focused on the door that it never occurs to me to bring them with me. In fact, I've never even thought to speak to them. When I go through the door, and it closes, does it lock them out? Do I leave them standing on the other side, locked out? Have they been reliving their own dream, over and over, only to watch me go through and leave them behind?

I couldn't stand it for another minute, so I went over to them and said, "You guys, the new door is unlocked now. Do you want to go through with me?"

They both smiled. Donna cocked an eyebrow and said, "Did you finally figure it out?"

"Figure it...huh?"

"Why you're here…did you work it out?"

"Um, kind of. The more I find out, the more questions I have, but hold on, you know what's going on?"

"Yes, we've been here before. In fact, you were with us."

"I was? When? Why don't I remember?"

"Because," she explained, "before, you were here to support us. Now, we're here to support you – and, those were our dreams. This is yours"

"So you're not coming with me?"

"Nope, this time is for you," my brother said, putting the lid on the Parcheesi box and looking calmly up at me.

I paused, and said sheepishly, "I thought I was being selfish leaving you both here. I didn't even think about bringing you before."

"You're not supposed to bring us, but now you've come to that thought, you might find that you can see some things more clearly," Ken replied.

"Sure you don't want to come?" I asked hesitantly.

"Some things you have to figure out on your own, bro."

Donna and Ken reached out and hugged me, and she said. "Go find it, little brother."

"Should I even ask what 'it' is?" I said.

"'It' is completely up to you." She replied."

I stood up, took a deep breath and walked through the door.

The door clicks shut behind me and I approach the table, thrilled to see that the book says "William" again, and it also has the date written under it – April 6, 1752. Yes! Progress! I turn the page to see if there is anything else, but the following pages are all blank. 1752, no wonder I couldn't think of who he is. He's not even from my time. He being from the distant past is really not going to make it easier, but the new information still feels like I'm getting somewhere. I give the room a quick look, but I don't see that anything else has changed

I'm so excited to tell Donna and Ken – I open the door back to the playroom, except it's not there. I've stepped into a strange room. It's sparsely populated with shabby furnishings and lit by a single guttering candle. A young man sits alone at a small desk, writing with an old-fashioned quill pen. He looks troubled and pauses frequently, staring at the page for long moments before continuing his writing. I watch him for what seems like a long time, and I feel a connection, but I don't recognize him. He's dressed in clean but threadbare clothing. There is a single trunk in the corner that looks as if it's in the last stages of being packed.

He finishes his writing, stands up, and looks around the room, then walks to his window and gazes at the little village outside. The framed photos on the top layer of the trunk, and the expression on his face make it seem like he is looking at his home for the very last time.

He drops the book into the trunk and carries it out the door, pausing to look around the room once more before closing it with a final click.

He has left no note.

Are we having fun yet?

"Guess who I saw last night."

"Who? William? Did you have another dream last night?" Steph is sitting on the edge of her chair. As usual, she's more excited about the details of my life than I am. Her gift for seeing the beauty in life, for never being too tired to be excited about seeing a little twinkle of joy, her intense strength and courage, it's those kinds of things that make me love and respect her so very much.

"You could say that, it was more like a flood. I saw him but I didn't really meet him. It looked like he was leaving to go somewhere, and it felt like a permanent move. He looked worried, like it was a major change in his life. I talked to Ken and Donna too for the first time in the dream; it explained a lot," I said. "It's actually getting a little scary..."

"How so?" she asked.

"Well, this is obviously not just my brain randomly stringing some dreams together. Something else is going on here," I said with some trepidation.

"Well, yes!"

"And, I'm not used to things like this happening." I said. "You're the one that's dialed in to the universe, not me. I've never been the one that has all the profound spiritual experience stories. At least not like this…"

"So what's the scary part?"

"The scary part is this is opening up so many things so fast that I'm having trouble digesting it all – and, I'm beginning to wonder what all is going to be expected of me."

"What has it cost you so far?" Stephanie asked reasonably.

"A lot of soul-searching, some of it not too enjoyable."

"And what have you gotten in return for it?" she said gently.

"More" I admitted.

"Does it feel right?"

"Yes, it feels right," I said, looking down at my hands, "and so does admitting you ran a stop sign when you get pulled over by a cop."

"But you know that's different."

"I do." I replied.

"Then there's something else?"

"I've come to realize there's always something else."

She let the silence work on me.

"I've relived some difficult things. I'm worried that there's more coming, and I'm not sure I want to go back there." I said with a growing lump in my throat.

"You told me you felt strong a really strong sense of resolution after you had the dream about Kate and her mom, right?"

"I did," I said honestly.

Silent thought again.

"Is there anything else you could use some resolution about?" she asked, already knowing the answer.

"That's what I'm afraid of."

Journal entry – July 28, 2019

I had a good talk with Steph about meeting William, and everything that comes with it. She helped pep me up a bit, but I'm still worried about what's coming next. I know she's right, but I still feel it looming out there. I'm trying to be still about it and accept what's coming. One of the things I've been given in this quest is the knowledge that if I don't handle the lesson well, I miss the whole point of the lesson. But then, Steph reminded me of a quote by Amelia Earhart, the famous pilot, "Use your fear...it can take you to a place where you store your courage."

730 Birch

60+ years on this spinning blue orb, and I can still tell you the address and phone number of the military quarters our family lived in when we moved to Alaska in the late 60s. I can quote the lyrics from numerous Frank Zappa songs that I haven't heard since before humans wore bell-bottoms. There are gazillions of bits of data floating around in my head, but I don't seem to have any control over which ones I retain and which are lost. Most I keep are just trivial things – a few are memories of tremendously wonderful or awful days in my life.

Unit 21-435, apartment A, Citrus Street conjures up summers of playing baseball in the big courtyard in front of our on-base apartment when my father was still in the Air Force. We had the run of the 13,000-acre military base, and life was simple and safe for big time hide-and-seek, miles-long bike rides and trout fishing in the local lakes. In the middle of summer Mom would call out to us that it was time to come in and get ready for bed and we'd cry out at the injustice of having to come in when it was still light out – at 11:00 pm (remember – Alaska, Land of the Midnight Sun). Our number was 753-7232. I could go on. But I won't. I know what this is leading up to and I don't want to go there. I feel like the character in a movie that forces himself to stay awake, because he knows the monster of his dreams comes in the night, but murky shadows are spreading and creeping across the ground with the coming darkness.

Through my heavy eyelids I see Jasmine, our little furry household guardian walking up to the bed. She lays her head down on my hand and looks at me with concern. As I lose my fight to stay awake, she curls up next to me on the floor, facing outward towards any possible menace.

. . .

I'm back in the stupid, noisy, shiny, vinyl beanbag chair again, and I'm alone. This is a cutting-edge, state-of-the-art, utopian playroom, intelligently designed to give me maximum comfort and peace of mind, and this is where I'm staying. I know what's coming next and I don't want it. I know exactly what happened in that room; I saw the evidence on the walls and on the carpet and everything else in there in such excruciatingly merciless detail that even after 45 years, there is nothing I could possibly gain from seeing it again.

I was 15 when I faced that door the first time, and I feel like I'm standing there again. A 15-year-old cannot just take the word of a cop bluntly telling him that his dad has killed himself. I didn't want to go through then either, but I did; I turned the handle myself and walked in. I was alone that day too. There was nobody to talk to. The rest of my family was somewhere else; I didn't know where they were or what they were doing. I had no idea my other family members were going through something far, far worse, as they had faced that door, before the official people had come.

I couldn't stay there very long; hopping on my bike, I rode as fast as I could to one of my friend's houses – then on to another's, and another's – until I found one of them at home. Most adults don't know what to say to a 15-year-old in that situation; another 15-year-old doesn't have much more of a chance. In fairness, I didn't know either. Standing still was torture, so I wound up leaving and riding around on my bike; I don't know for how long, I just wanted to keep moving. I remember spending most of the time screaming inside, and marveling at the way the rest of the world was completely ignorant of my situation, and wishing I were one of them. When your world stops, it feels like the rest of the world should know, and stop with you, but it doesn't. Cars drive by, people sit reading on the porch, the radio still plays pre-recorded hits; and it happens everywhere, every day. Maybe it has to be that way. Maybe nobody else can see what we see, the way we see it.

I'm not going. I am not going.
The door opens by itself – slowly, apologetically.
"Please stop," I whisper.
I can see the warm light coming from it.
I look away mutinously. I didn't ask for this, I just wanted to know who the hell William was. And then I find that I'm no longer sitting down, instead, I'm now standing by the table – the door clicks shut behind me.
So I don't even have a choice?

I refuse to look down at the book. I just stand there, rigid, looking out the window. Outside, the field and harbor are as beautiful as before, but I can't care. My heart is curled up naked and sobbing as I watch that same lonely ship, still bucking the tide, still working its way up the channel, still fighting to make it to the safety and peace of the harbor. My anger has me shaking my head at the ship, thinking, why do you even bother?

A still, small voice whispers to me, not with words, but with knowledge. I don't have to look at the book if I don't want to. Moments pass. I haven't looked down, but I feel love radiating from the book, just as I could feel the warm sun on my face the last time I was here.

So I do have a choice.

The open page says 730 Birch, just like I knew it would – the address of our house, where I lost my father to suicide.

Now I have to turn around and face the door.

It opens by itself again, but it isn't the door I was afraid of. It's looking out onto the field where I saw Kate and her mother. I'm drawn outside again and start to walk down the lane that crosses the field. A little further down I see a man I know, peacefully walking along hand-in-hand with me, as a little boy.

Dad. He's okay.

Again, there is no darkness. There's just golden light and love. The same swaying sea grass dances with the gentle wind, and they walk down the lane through the field, and the vision fades.

. . .

"Morning hon, sleep good?" Steph says with a yawn.

I manage to choke out, "I did."

Resolution. Thank you.

The day my father died was the day I changed my perspective of the word "fair." Since then I've believed there is only one thing that can be truly fair in the world: the fact that sooner or later, everyone suffers. The amount of suffering varies from one person to the next, and so does each person's ability to endure it. Today I'll have to amend that belief to allow for what comes later; each of us has the opportunity to find relief from our pain. I'll also have to make a big, bold mental note to remember what I felt like that day on my bike, when nobody that I saw knew what I was going through, and keep it in mind whenever I see someone who looks like their world has just stopped.

I know I'll have to hold off a couple days before speaking to anyone about this latest dream. Not because it's too painful, but because I'm still going over it in my mind, and I don't want to lose any of the details. Revisiting the dream is like walking through the field again – it still exists in multiple dimensions in my mind, with every bit as much precision. My walk through the field was short, but there is so much more coming back to me than I thought I had time to see – the look of peace on my father's face, the laughter on my young face looking up to him; like he was getting to raise me again, but free of the darkness he had felt in life. I was even seeing, or sensing some of those same feelings as I sat at home, looking out my window thinking about the dream. The trees outside my window seemed to be moving more than they should in the light airs, like they were trying to say something to me. The more I watched them, the more I could almost understand what they were saying.

I felt only love, and time; and the curiosity is here too – me for the field, the field for me.

And resolution.

The Woodstove Channel

The woodstove is warmed up, and the birch log fire inside has taken on the look of a windowed kiln – somewhere between red- and white-hot – smoke-free, with more than enough heat to keep the large glass door clean and clear. It's still early enough that I haven't had to wake up from the sound of cooling metal, quietly ticking to let me know it's time to stoke the fire.

The first night at the cabin is always the one we enjoy the most, and still feel the "I can't believe we finally made it back " moment again. We knew the family cabin was the place to be after the busy weeks we just put behind us, and I knew privately that I was in need of a break from the emotional flood that had swept in. I figure if I'm getting up four times a night to stoke the woodstove I won't be taking too many forays into dreamland.

Watching the firelight caper around the exposed ceiling timbers is usually a good way to fall back into slumber, but tonight it just calms me and lets me coast mentally; not focused on anything but the fact that we're warm and dry and there's no phone to interrupt the quiet. It's one of those times when having a blank mind is much the same as thinking. Nothing is in the forefront, but I can feel the back room crew quietly processing what I saw and learned in my vision of my dad.

We didn't do too much today; like most winter trips, after the 25-mile snowmobile ride in, I spent the usual two or three hours shoveling the paths to the outhouse and woodshed, so necessaries would be accessible. By then, dinner and warm, dry clothes are all I need to put up my feet, and watch the flames on what I like to call, *The Woodstove Channel.*

About 3:00 am I hear the familiar ticking sound, so I know it's time to put another log on the fire. It's dark enough that I can see the sunset glow behind the mountain – and then I remember, it's 3:00 am, the sunset is long gone – and the sunset glow is green. There are no nuclear power plants in Alaska, which means green tinges on the horizon are from the Aurora.

I put a couple pieces of split birch on the fire and lie down on my back on the window seat cushions and watch the sky shimmer. Legend says you can whistle at the Northern Lights to make them dance around – it has never worked for me. We're 25 miles away from the nearest town, so the sky is dark, and the stars are popping. There was a cold spell the weeks before, and the ice fog stripped most of the dust from the air; it's so clear the stars hardly even sparkle, and even the Milky Way is visible.

My brain is content to just drift around and track the moon until it sets behind the mountain, and then I sleep. We wake up to the first pink washes crossing the east face of Mt. Susitna. A young bull moose was down on the frozen creek grazing in the willows, indifferent to the painterly sunrise hues. It strikes me how the moose has no idea how majestic it looks to me, it just goes about the business of living, not even knowing that I am watching it, like I watch people that I love and respect – the people who teach me.

The first rule of cabin life is that the chores are never done. The silver lining is that because they are never done, it's ok not to stress about it, and to take a break once in a while. There is always time for sleeping in, reading, and the other things we specifically built the cabin to do. Today's chore to-do list was fluid. We had plenty of firewood split, no major repairs to make, and we just felt like recharging. After an iconic Alaska breakfast of hotcakes, eggs, and Spam, I refilled the bird feeders, and we climbed up on the window seat with too many pillows and settled in, each with a book.

A couple hours and a nap later we put on our winter gear for a ride down the creek to visit friends and check on the progress of their cabin projects. Visiting always makes the clock move too fast. Before we know it, we've been riding around the creek for a few hours and the sun has almost completed its shallow winter arc over the southern horizon (something Alaskans are used to), so we head back to our cabin to build up the fire again and start thinking about dinner. Everything tastes better at the cabin, so we could be lazy and enjoy a plain meal, but Steph loves to make everything she touches a little better, so I'm in for another treat. While she's finishing it up I step outside to fire up the generator, since it'll be dark soon. It's February, which means the longer daylight hours are coming back, but it'll still be dark by 5:00 or so, and lights and dinner with a movie sound like just the ticket.

Later that night, I went out to shut off the generator for the night, and as I was standing in the dark letting my eyes adjust, I heard a little skittering sound pass by me. I stood still listening, but didn't hear it anymore, so I switched my headlamp on and saw two glowing eyes looking back at me. They were only a few inches apart, and low to the ground, so I knew that it wasn't anything too dangerous. As it turned sideways, I could see that it was a red fox, probably searching for scraps. I whistled like I was calling a dog, and he perked up and took a couple steps towards me. I figured it must be one of the local critters that made the rounds to all the cabins in the area, so we put together a little snack of Spam and leftover chicken and left it on the porch for him – something we only do in winter, when the larger furry brown things are in their deep slumber. I said good night to our visitor and went in for another night of mostly dreamless sleep. The next morning the food and the fox were gone. Little encounters like that, and watching our little flocks that frequent the bird feeders are a couple of the simple joys of being out there in the woods. Nature has a way of curing our ills while we're not looking.

Snow Day! This morning we woke up to a curtain of white outside our window. City folk can only pretend to know what a snow day is. The middle of a forest hundreds of square miles in size is the place to experience the hush of billions of tufty snowflakes falling silently, covering everything in a thick blanket and rounding off the square corners of the world. It's a rule that the only thing allowed on snow days is food and puzzles, and a crackling fire of course. Music is optional.

A couple evenings later I was sitting in front of the woodstove again. Steph reclined on the bed reading her book, and I was about half awake staring at the fire, watching flames chase each other around, playing tag on the logs. A thought came to me about my two visits to the field where I saw Kate and her mom, and my dad and me. I had been thinking that the magical moment in both encounters was that I had brought a gift of knowledge back with me. This new thought was different. It occurred to me that the key wasn't what I was able to take with me. It was what I was able to leave there. The knowledge didn't fix me. It just allowed me to let go of the dark things I had been holding onto. It was resolution, more complete than I had realized.

The day we like least is the day we have to go back to town, and as we rode away I had to wonder if the cabin (or the moose) would miss us too. That thought will make a good closing to my next journal entry.

Search and Rescue

On the way home I was thinking about what an OCD planner I am. As an example, every trek we take is preceded by days of making notes and mentally reviewing the upcoming trip plans in extreme detail. I do it so we're prepared, because we have survived a few surprises that could have gone either way, in large part because we were ready for them, mentally and physically; the mental preparation being the most important part of any backcountry excursion, because there are always surprises.

Today my random journal-opening method took me back to one of those surprises we encountered on a fall trip in 2007. We were taking our jet boat on the 30-mile run from the Deshka Landing down the Susitna River to the cabin. Susitna means "sandy river" in the indigenous Dena'ina language of the region. It's aptly named, as it is a shallow, braided, and very powerful river, which cuts a ragged swath through the natural gravel pit that is the Matanuska/Sustina Valley. The Susitna is the main drainage for the MatSu Valley, but its main source is melt water from Susitna Glacier, over 300 miles to the north, which feeds it enough to make it the 15th largest river by volume in the U.S. The sheer volume of fast-moving water carves the hills away, leaving crumbling gravel cut banks on nearly every bend in the river, pulling large trees into the current as it eats away at the riverbanks.

Big rivers are dynamic by nature and this one changes daily. The rainfall that winds up in hundreds of feeder streams, together with fluctuating temperatures at the glacier, can make the river levels rise or fall several feet daily. The wildlife varies as much as the waterline. Brown and black bears, moose, wolves, fox, and many species of fish and birds populate the rich valley, and give us plenty to watch for. Seals follow the salmon up into the river in the summer and we often see them hauled out on sandbars, basking in the sun. Hooligan, a type of smelt, take to the river to spawn in such numbers that it seems like every predator in the valley visits the river's edge to gorge on them.

On the day of this particular surprise, we were navigating through a particularly wide section of the river, just south of the confluence of the Susitna and Yentna rivers, when we noticed a bright yellow Piper Super Cub floatplane approaching us on a converging course. Seeing airplanes in Alaska's Bush is commonplace, so I didn't think anything of it. As we got closer to each other, he began to descend towards us. I thought we either knew them, or they were just buzzing us for fun. The airplane dived down to about 50 feet, waggled its wings, and passed over us – immediately peeling off, banking to the right and settling on a straight course towards a group of islands in the middle of the river.

After a few moments, they banked right and climbed, turning again until they lined up on us for a second pass, then dived down low again, turning to the same heading to the islands. About the time they were beginning a third cycle of this pattern, I realized that this wasn't just someone saying hello on their way to their cabin. They were sending us a message, so I turned the boat towards the islands. This time they buzzed us and then kept flying in the same straight course, passing very low between the first and second island. Sure enough, as we came around the corner we found a stranded boat, high-centered on a sandbar close to the island. It was late in the season and they had picked an out-of-the-way spot to get stuck. Even when the river is busy in mid-summer, there is very little traffic by the islands since most river runners know it's not usually navigable there.

The stranded boat, like most that run the Susitna River, was a jet boat. Instead of having a propeller pushing it through the water, it uses the motor's power to force water through an impeller, which shoots a powerful jet of out the back end of the boat. The reason for using a jet over a prop is that you can travel through much shallower water. The downside is that when you get stuck, you get stuck worse, because you' re typically moving through less than twelve inches of water.

To complicate the predicament, the boat they were in was about twice the weight of our boat so I knew it wasn't going to be easy to free them from the bar, but we had to give it a try, because nobody else would be coming. After an hour or more of pulling with our boat, and six people pushing and rocking it, we were able to slide it back into deeper water and wound up with a happy ending.

This is one of the main reasons Alaskans love Alaska. Our state covers 500,000 square miles of wildly rugged country and sooner or later, everyone needs help, so as a rule, most of us try to watch out for each other, especially out in remote bush areas of Alaska. Because the pilot signaled us, and we stopped, we were able to combine our efforts and help the stranded boat. That jet boat driver was lucky there was somebody up there looking out for him.

Putting my journal down, I'm left with the distinct impression that somebody up there is buzzing me to help me find William. At the same time, I feel like it might be more than a one-hour detour to find him.

Go Fish

*J*ournal entry – September 19, 2019

I made the right decision to start writing in my journal again. I was worried that it would be a distraction, but it's proved the opposite. I've been slowly gaining surety. It's tough to describe. It's not like I'm magically finding answers to my problems, but I do feel like I'm being steered a little towards the solutions I'm hoping for. If it's magic, it's subtle magic. I would use the "bird whispering in my ear" expression if it weren't for my past experiences with Bob the Bird. I'm not letting him anywhere near my ear. Still, I don't feel as if I'm stumbling around as blindly as I had been.

Every time I hear an airplane, which in Alaska is almost daily, I jerk my head around to see if the yellow Cub is trying to get my attention again, but so far all the airplanes have been attending to their own business. And really, things like that usually only happen once. So instead, I'm trying again to follow my artist's rule of learning to look harder to see more clearly, and one thing that's clear is that every scene is different and has to be approached individually.

The trip to the cabin was well needed, and I feel recharged. It's always a chore to get there because something always seems to come up to keep us away. But that always happens whenever we start something good. There must be opposition, right? Otherwise we don't learn, or appreciate things as much. I get it, but sometimes it ranks right up there with growth opportunities.

That's enough journal writing for today. I'm clamoring to get back to the old pictures Steph found today. We've been actively engaged in trying to bring the house into better order, including cleaning up a crawlspace that has been the dumping ground for "things we might need," for 34 years. If you're a Harry Potter fan, picture a smallish Room of Requirement.

It's not all junk though, we've been discovering things that we still consider very valuable, like the boxes filled with family photos. The last batch found was from the 80s, our college years: sitting by the pool, walking around ASU campus, tubing on the Salt River. Mixed in with those were some photos I didn't remember taking during my years of commercial fishing with Steph's dad in Bristol Bay, Alaska. Commercial fishing is how I paid for my education, and more importantly, it's where I learned how to work – with my father-in-law (one of my four fathers) in the place of headmaster at the school of hard knocks. He learned there as well, when he fished in a double-ender sailboat in the 50s, without all the luxuries we had: diesel power, electronic navigation aids, hydraulic reels, and a cabin to stay warm in. The only camera I had to record my time there was an old Minolta 110 Instamatic – the kind of 70s technology that used film with frames about as big as the nail on my pinky. Something about the poor image quality is nice, though – it dates the images, and the memories feel more nostalgic when they look ancient (by today's smartphone standards).

I say we fished in Bristol Bay, but specifically we worked in Nushagak Bay, one of the western districts between Togiak Bay and the easternmost districts clustered in the Naknek area. Nushagak Bay gets its name from the Nushagak River that feeds the bay (along with the Wood River), and flows from the richest sport fishing region in the world. A good season meant we could expect in excess of 35 million fish to pass through the whole of the Bristol Bay area. Working on the fish boat was a far cry from the $2,000-a-day sport fishing lodges that operated upriver from where we spent our long summer days. But we did get to see what 10,000 lbs. of sockeye salmon look like hitting a 900-foot-long gillnet – and what they look like coming over the roller onto the deck, kicking and fighting all the way. We also got to see an old Alaska Native man, that we really didn't know, alone in his old wooden boat, cruising back and forth to watch over us, the day we were stranded at low tide on the Long Sands – a treacherous bar in mid-channel.

Nushagak Bay is a curving, horn-shaped body of water about 40 miles long, divided by several massive sandbars created by the unimaginable tidal forces that pass through it four times a day. We had gotten sucked into a shallow gut between two sections of the miles-long bar by a vicious rip current, leaving us aground at low tide. Our predicament would have wound up much more serious if not for the quick thinking of our skipper, who, seconds after we first bumped along the bottom, started the engine and firewalled the throttle to point our bow into the wind, just as we settled onto the hard bottom of the bay. Within minutes we were high and dry, surrounded by rough shore-break from the southwesterly winds that were pushing waves up the bay. A few more minutes and we were hundreds of feet from the water's edge.

We spent the next six hours picking the fish out of the nets, rinsing sand off the 5,000 lbs. of salmon in the remaining puddles of standing water, then rinsing the nets and stowing everything in the hold. We had a short time left before the incoming tide made it back to us, so we used that time to add extra anchor line and bury the anchor deep in the sand. It was the quickest, most frantic six hours of my life.

While we watched and waited in the boat for the first pounding waves of the incoming tide, we noticed the old Native man cruising just offshore. He had pulled in his nets – during the peak of the fishing season – to make sure we made it off the bar without foundering or being beaten apart by the surf. The skipper's foresight six hours earlier saved the day. As the water level rose and the waves started to pound the boat, we began to float, and the waves picked us up and straightened us out, bow-first into the oncoming surf. Thirty minutes later our nets were back in the water, with splashes up and down the floating cork line making dollar signs in our eyes.

In the years I spent fishing in the bay I must have had someone else occasionally taking pictures with my camera, because one of the happier photos caught me in my dirty, canary-yellow Helly Hansen slickers, holding up two nice, fat king salmon. You can tell it's mid-season in the photo because of my Three Musketeers-style beard, festooned with sparkly fish scales – the fisherman's fashion glitter.

My years on "The Fish Boat" were pivotal in my coming of age – the growth opportunity of all growth opportunities – some of the most uncomfortable and difficult months of my life, barring death in the family, but also some of the most meaningful. There is nothing to make you feel alive that compares with being cold, wet, and dirty, working like a madman on a small boat in a violent sea, one mistake away from maybe not going home. In those years I heard a number of panic-stricken radio broadcasts; one skipper screaming, "Man overboard," another crying out that a 50-foot right whale had become tangled in his nets and was hauling him backwards through the sea, with water coming in over his transom. That day we were fortunate and made it off the sandbar in one piece, but every season somebody drowned, boats sank or burned – someone didn't make it home. The ones that did took with them strength, hard-earned money, and a lifetime of memories. It was my personal version of *Deadliest Catch*.

The striking contrast is that the day after a life and death situation I could find myself sitting, bone-tired on the hatch covers after making the delivery at a normal day's end, getting my daily massage from leaning against the warm, vibrating engine exhaust stack, watching the sun set on a placid evening – not desiring anything else. There was a particular day when a pod of almost a hundred brilliantly white beluga whales passed us, chasing salmon up the bay. We had a towering wall of black clouds in front of us and the sunset's elongated rays blasting us from behind, making their white bodies glow in the brown tidal waters as if they were lit from within.

After a few years, I was able to understand why people fall in love with a life at sea. It holds the most mild gentleness, and at the same time a power so impossibly immense that I can't imagine it could ever be adequately described, even using every word and emotion ever presumed by humanity.

But I didn't take that many pictures so you'll have to take my word for it, or go fish.

The Noon Bell

Looking through the boxes of old photos was the highlight of our week. It was such a hit that we wound up pulling out more boxes and made a night out of it – our lives flashing before our eyes in the best possible way. All the kids (now adults) gathered around, and we passed the photo packets around, trying to keep the pictures matched up with their own envelopes and negatives.

To me, pictures are just a different kind of journal. They may not explain details as well as the written word, but you can't beat them for capturing the feeling of a moment. The pictures of our kids lie there spread out on the carpet, and still shout, "Look at me, Mommy and Daddy!" Seeing all of our younger selves makes me feel so much more complete. At times I lose touch of who I was at the different stages of my life; as a baby, toddler, kid, teen, and young man, and family photo nights help me get a little bit of that back, and provide a good laugh for the kids. Oh my, the 70s; I didn't remember bell-bottoms being so huge, or how long my hair used to be.

It's funny, the time spans are different, but it's the same feeling of connection I used to get when I was looking back into our family history, searching through old historical archives to find long-lost relatives. I find the separation of the years doesn't dull that connection or make it any different in nature. The first time I went into the new room I described the feeling there as curiosity, but my different choice of words doesn't alter the connected feeling I'm talking about. Maybe it's a curiosity we can't help feeling about who we all were and are, and how we connect to each other – wondering how our ancestors spent their days and what they cared about, and were afraid of. Maybe we're hard-wired to crave the connection because the connection makes us whole. I feel that a little every day when I go home and ask Steph how she spent her day, and now, when I think about William. I want to know because I care, and I care because I know. It's a thought that stays with me until my head hits the pillow.

. . .

Walking through the door I find myself in a dark space. Actually, it's dark and damp, with a constant din of creaking and groaning, and an overwhelming reek that's a combination of too many foul odors to be described by one name. Stacks of crates, barrels, trunks and hundreds of other unidentifiable items are packed so tightly that they are barely outlined by the weak light that finds its way into the cramped space. I can hear a low rumble of furtive conversation from behind a nearby bulkhead; it's obvious by the corkscrew pitching motion that I'm in the hold of a very old ship.

I move towards the voices and come to an open door. A man sitting on a small bunk closes a book and lays it down gently. He rises and steps out of the tiny cabin and walks unsteadily down the passage, to the end of a gangway where a steep ladder disappears into a bright square of light framed by an open hatch. He climbs out and leans against the mast, blinking and wiping tears from his eyes as they adjust to the harsh sunlight blazing on the brig's weather deck. His gaze sweeps around from horizon to horizon, finding nothing but deep blue water flecked with white foam on the tips of the unending procession of waves they are plowing through. The sky is clear, not a puff of a cloud or even a solitary bird to break the continuous field of color overhead. No birds; that means they are still far out to sea, even after six weeks of sailing. The crew has the resigned look of men consigned to the unbroken ritual between ports. With the exception of a few inconsequential squalls, the vessel has been driven along by the trade winds that have ensured an endless cycle of long watches on deck, with hardly a need for trimming a sail, only interrupted at the noon bell for the taking of sightings with the sextant.

The way William stares out at the roiling ocean swell, I sense he's been doing it every day since boarding. He has the same the look of guarded curiosity he had when he took his last look from the window of his home months ago. All his possessions had barely enough value to secure him passage on the brig, and steerage class at that. He was not a gambling man – but he did not think this was a gamble, neither was it a sure thing – but he had an undeniable impression that this journey was meant to be, and faith that it would be successful. So he keeps coming out on deck every day so as to not miss the thing he expects to see. He knows there is something new out there. He isn't sure what it is, but he knows he has to make the attempt. It's why he left the only home he knew, he had to find the answer.

The captain, who has been pacing the deck, motions for William to join him on the sacred windward side of the quarterdeck, where none can tread without his invitation. The two men appear to return to an ongoing conversation they have been having about the differences between living at sea and life ashore. The captain, who has spent all of his adult life and much of his childhood far offshore, seems never to suffer from a want of advice and opinions, and appears to be pleasant company for William.

Their discussion is momentarily interrupted by a junior officer who approaches to discuss a navigational matter with the captain, and William looks over the stern rail and sees the straight, unbroken line of the wake behind the ship – fervently hoping that the forces steering his course are as sure and steady as the hand on the ship's wheel. He would take to the deck again tomorrow morning and look again.

. . .

I usually make journal entries at the end of the day. This one won't wait.

Journal entry – November 6, 2019 – 7:30 am

Okay, that was vivid. Years ago Steph read a compilation of stories written by people who had been through near-death experiences. The individuals' accounts almost universally described out-of-body views that were extremely realistic, with almost palpable sensations of serenity, warmth, and security.

I just felt those distinctive characteristics, except fortunately nobody told me to walk towards the light. It was so strong that I'm wondering if I'm the subject of one of those "I see dead people" storylines where the protagonist doesn't realize that they're dead. I pinched my arm to see if I was awake, but as real as that dream felt, I'm not confident that's a proper test. I'm going ahead with the assumption that I am still alive, because my back hurts and I have morning breath.

So, William is leaving home, but where is he going? His clothes, the old ship, his quill pen, all the details in the dream leave me certain that this happened a long time ago, confirming the date in the book. William must have lived at least a couple hundred years ago, and I'm seeing his story across the span of time. Except for those visual cues, though, watching him doesn't lead me to think he's much different than someone living today, apart from being more courageous. Maybe he's left to find his fortune or to escape some kind of loss or persecution. It was something profound; the look on his face in his home was resolute, unwavering, like there was great risk involved and great faith required.

I still don't know who he is, but I'm excited for William, and not just to see more of his story. Watching him advancing towards something big is like watching one of our kids progressing with their education or launching a new career. From my perspective it looks like his course is true.

It'll be Ready When it's Ready

My family and Mark are still the only people I've talked to about what's been happening. This extracurricular excursion has been such a personal and peculiar phenomenon that I've hesitated to share it. I delayed speaking to the kids about it for a while, but they know me; to them it probably seems like just another example of Dad "thinking out loud."

Every time I've thought about opening up to someone about it, I've heard my brother saying, *"Some things you have to figure out on your own, bro."* It hasn't been easy for me, since I've never been one to keep things so close in the past; in fact I have a tough time keeping most thoughts in my head. I really should always go around wearing a T-shirt with "Did I just say that out loud?" printed across the chest.

To fall back on another artist's characterization, this experience is feeling very much like a painting that's not yet ready to show. The basic design and base color have been blocked in, but you can't tell what the finished product is going to look like, and if you did peek, it would be disappointing. Remember when I tried to portray the dynamics of watercolor painting? Well, in this painting I would be at the point where the pigment is swirling around, and I'm still trying to figure out how much to work it with my brush, and how much to let it settle on its own. It's the watercolorist's dilemma, and it is usually the difference between a thing of beauty and a waste of time. And I sense that this is far too important to rush it and cause it to be the latter.

At this point in a painting, it pays off big time to think first, work one area at a time, and give it some freedom to settle in its own time and place (just like life, oddly enough). Whenever I've applied that technique, I've found success. I feel strongly that this last big revelation about William added some important details that will define the final piece, even if I can't see it yet. Just like a journal – line upon line, precept upon precept. I'm starting to get a picture in my mind of where this is heading, but it won't be ready to frame, until it's ready.

So I'll keep talking to my journal and Steph, my favorite pal and confidant, and keep working it until it's finished. Maybe then it'll be worth sharing.

Journal entry – January 20, 2020

Thinking about William's Excellent Adventure and what it all means. If the name Ted pops up in the book, this is really going to get weird.

Learning, growing old, sharing lives, watching kids grow up, working on a career, finding what your passion is – we can't see any of it entirely from the front end – most of those things are a lifetime of work, and we can usually only see it clearly when we view it from the other end, when all the pieces are finally in place. Is this why all the important things in life are so hard? And, why it takes most of our lives to finally have a clear picture and understanding of how life works? Hindsight really is 20/20.

A truth related to this was demonstrated to me one fine summer day in the early 80s. I was with a group of friends on the Kenai River, the place to go to fish for the world's biggest king salmon, when after a day of combat fishing (shoulder-to-shoulder on the riverbank), we agreed just before dusk that it was time to start back to our campsite at the Lower Russian River Campground. The daylight hours of Alaska summers are long, but it was getting fairly gloomy under the thick canopy of old-growth spruce trees, so we knew returning sooner would be better than later. The five of us got packed up and were hiking along the worn trail at the top of the cut bank at the confluence of the Russian and the Kenai, when we were approached by another, larger group; they were going the same direction as us and had seen that we were carrying a flashlight – something they neglected to bring. By the time we talked over the route with them and started walking into the darkening woods, we really needed the flashlight to see where to go.

Earlier in the day, there had been a very big, very friendly black Lab romping around the riverbank, getting chummy with everyone and sniffing everyone's catch on their stringers. I was the fifth soul back in a marching line of an even dozen, and I could just see the big happy doggo bounding up the trail, right towards my friend, Robert, our point man with the flashlight. Because the dog was so dark, and Robert was looking at the brightly lit trail, he didn't see the dog approaching, until the moment he jumped up and put his paws suddenly and squarely in the middle of Robert's chest. I hadn't warned him because I assumed he had seen the dog running up. Robert's first thought was "black bear", which was followed with a loud and rapid-fire exclamation that would do a longshoreman proud. We had covered all of 100 yards and were still close to people fishing on the riverbank, who were all wondering what a dozen young hikers were screaming about (but none of them stopped fishing). A couple minutes later the nervous laughter had settled down, and we set out again.

By now it was pitch black by Alaska summer standards and we were making our way down the trail at a snail's pace, thinking about toothy animals bursting out of the shadows. Robert, still the point man (it was his flashlight) was calmly calling out "root...stump...branch" to warn everyone behind what was coming next on the trail. Each person would in turn repeat the warning, all down the line of 12 hikers, which sounded like an exceptionally tone-deaf camp choir. I think I was the only person in our strange troop that had a firearm – a handy item for the Alaska backcountry – but it wasn't terribly necessary with the combined voices of a dozen people chanting and stomping down a trail, sounding like some unearthly monster to the poor bruins that I'm sure were hiding in the bushes. Besides that, trying to aim a large-caliber pistol at a rapidly charging animal in a large group in the middle of the night would be a recipe for disaster. It's not a long trail, but it did take us quite a while to make it all the way to the campground, with the splashing river on our right the whole way to keep us company, (and mask out the worrisome sound of any critters potentially tracking alongside us). We reached our destination safe and sound, and the merry band split up, each to our respective campsites.

The experience was something of an allegory to leadership, guidance, and trust that has stayed with me all this time. Only one person in our wandering band could see the trail, and then only for a few yards by the weak light of the flashlight. But each time he stepped into the light, the beam washed over new ground, and revealed a little more of the trail, so he could pass on what he saw to the person behind him, with the rest of us doing the same, all the way down the line. We had no idea what we would find along our trail, but we kept taking each step, because we knew we could do that much at the very least. This simple practice took us safely through the rough trail in the dark of night, and I've tried all my life to practice it and another strategy that works hand-in-hand – walk into the light as far as you can see, and you'll always be able to see a little further; and, learn good things from good people, and pass them on.

Comfortable Genes

I'm quite blessed to have a very creative family. Everyone in our home is artistically inclined in some way – some as artists, some with musical talent, some are creative in the kitchen, others in the garden (most with a few of these talents), and one as an inventor in his own right. The interesting thing is that we all see things in different ways and come up with different solutions for any given problem. I think that's one of the miraculous traits of humanity. There are billions of us swarming the planet, but each of us is an individual. In my art classes in college the students were frequently assigned the task of drawing a still life setting to practice visualizing and illustrating different shapes. Walking around the room afterwards revealed how each person's results varied widely. This is partly because we were all viewing the setting from different directions, but also because we saw it differently through our own eyes, and the way we chose to illustrate it, or tell its story. There is tremendous value in our differences. We form councils because there is wisdom in considering the opinions of others, and it teaches us the worth that every person has.

In the past I've had a habit of discounting that value because of the disconnect I felt from people who lived so long ago and so far away, but the recent interest I've found with William has closed that gap for me, and I find myself longing to find out more about his life and his dreams, from his perspective.

Perspective is a marvelous thing. It's what allows us to see ways to walk around barriers.

I began studying perspective as a drawing technique when I was young. Perspective drawing is all about representing objects in three-dimensions as they appear to us in real life. It's the way objects that are further away seem to be smaller, and lines that we know to be parallel appear to converge over distance. The drawing technique involves using horizon lines, vanishing points, projections and other means to accurately portray the shapes of things that our minds accept as correct and proper.

Random Trivia Moment: the ancient Greeks took this thought much further by distorting reality so it would appear more correct. The most famous example of this is the Parthenon, probably the most recognizable piece of architecture in Greek history. The Parthenon sits atop the Acropolis in Athens, where the Gods were said to have dwelt. The Parthenon was dedicated to the Goddess Athena and also served as the city treasury. For the time, it was a colossal structure, measuring 228 by 101 feet. Art historians teach that there is not a straight line in the entire design. The columns are tapered and all tilt slightly inward, and the entire roof structure is slightly curved, which allows rainwater to shed, but also serves a more subtle purpose. The architects of the Parthenon designed it that way because they understood that when someone looked at it from the city, below the Acropolis, the curvature of their eye would make the straight lines appear curved, much the same way a camera lens can distort an image – all for the sake of perspective.

Perspective is everything. It's even taught me the meaning of other words, like attitude. Even though I knew of its secondary definition, I've always thought about attitude as the way you feel about something; I've been told more than once that I needed a better attitude. But until I thought about it from the perspective of a pilot, I didn't fully appreciate it. Technically, attitude is the angular difference measured between an airplane's axis and the line of the earth's horizon. Simply put, it's what direction you're looking at something – from your perspective. And your perspective changes drastically depending on how close you are to something, and whether the object (or person) of your scrutiny is above you, or beneath you – literally and figuratively speaking.

From a distance, standing water can look like an impassable barrier, but up close you may be surprised to find that it's only an inch deep. A better attitude towards an uncomfortable problem, by that definition, can remove a lot of the negative emotion of a situation, even change the way you feel about something or someone. My perspective of William has changed since I began to see him. I don't know that much about him, but it's enough to see some of the qualities he possesses. This new perspective has not only changed my view of him, it's changing me in profound ways.

In the future I will most certainly try to utilize my creative genes, and check my perspective (and attitude) whenever I'm looking at a problem, or a person.

I Could Just Spit

Yesterday I was reading in my old journals, and came across an entry about the delight I felt in finding a long-lost relative after a prolonged search in historical records. I don't recall what his name was, but I remember he was one of my family's first ancestors to come to America. There is a magical feeling in finding your kindred, especially when you can find their stories along the way.

One of my uncles has had a strong interest in our family genealogy for many years. He compiled and published our family tree as it stood in the 1970s, and included a couple of marvelous things on the design – a small map showing the location of the original family homestead and a story about an old grandfather clock (affectionately known as Betty). One of our ancestors purchased the clock "in the week of Perry's victory," near Erie, Pennsylvania, during the War of 1812. The text gives an account of the order of possession of the clock in a couple of informal but charming paragraphs, including a mention (with curious spelling) that a case for the clock was "hughed out of a cherry log." I don't know who Hugh was, but it sounds like it hurt. About 100 years after its original purchase, another family member received an offer to sell it to the Ford Foundation Museum, which he refused. My uncle has the clock to this day, and it still functions, although he doesn't use it, as it could damage its internal workings if it were wound, and it would lose a couple hours a day if it were kept in operation with its original mechanism.

To me, a 200-year old clock that still works is a statement of the high level of creativity, dedication and craftsmanship that was present when it was created. We flatter ourselves that our day and age is vastly superior because of the level of technology that we enjoy, but I'm not so sure our lives are better because of it. For all that we have, we are on average less healthy, more dependent on our "superior" devices, and I would say less happy. People spend great amounts of time and money to escape their lives so they can get back to nature and "the simple life," and sometimes dream they could live like that daily. Our amazing new inventions certainly make it possible for us to do more than we used to, but is more always better? Natural gas heating is comfortable and consistent, but when I chop wood to fuel our woodstove, I appreciate the heat much more because of the effort it cost me. Hand-writing a letter takes much more time than sending a message electronically, but writing by hand lets me think more about what I'm saying, and receiving a written letter means more, because I know someone took the time to do it, for me. As quiet and simple as it is, there are few things more beautiful than a well-penned, hand-written letter from one loved one to another. A text message just doesn't say it the same way. We push ourselves so hard for most of our lives, often yearning for a different kind of existence, and we rarely stop to weigh the cost to individuals, families and communities.

I've found that the secret balance is to value the new discoveries, but also not to forget the worth of taking the time to spend our effort the best way we can, even if it costs us more time and energy, because sometimes the doing of the thing is the lesson, and the reward. We climb a mountain to get to the top, but the exercise and joy happen on the way there.

I've been thinking about getting back into family history again, maybe because of my reentry into journal writing. It's changed drastically since the days when I was actively involved. Just a few short years ago I spent hours scrolling through microfiche films, looking through alphabetically listed rolls of birth, wedding, and death records. Today, most everything is computerized and cross-referenced; records are all in the Cloud, and it's faster and much more convenient. My daughter even gave the whole family membership in a DNA-based program that links you genetically to people you may not be able to find on paper, and all you have to do is send them a little vial of spit. I love that it makes it so easy to share the information that we gather, and I appreciate what it does for the tasks I'm doing, so I use it for the work that is so important to me. But I'm still going to visit the old records from time-to-time, because I never want to lose the personal attachment to the souls I'm searching for.

Sea Change

W*illiam*

Day 56 - Today marks the end of our eighth week at sea. We had expected to complete our journey by this time but weeks of unfavorable winds and contrary currents have slowed our progress. The captain has long since shifted cargo in the hold to achieve the best distribution of weight and give the vessel the most efficient sailing trim, but still we press on, laboring against wind and water. Even now the crew makes frequent adjustments to the sails to catch every breath of wind possible.

We have been so long at sea that I find myself becoming used to this life. The never-ending routine of the sailors' activities are a comfort to me, when I might otherwise be disquieted by the realization of how small and vulnerable we are, bobbing like a tiny cockleshell on this infinite sea. The whistles and tramping of feet every few hours as the watch changes, the ceaseless trimming of the sails, the captain's habitual pacing of the quarterdeck, even the occasional peaceful nights when the crew gathers on deck to sing and dance, combine to make it seem that I came to be on this ship, and that it has been the sum of my existence. It may be that this is true metaphorically. I cannot say that I am the same person I was when I commenced this journey. As I review the thoughts, dreams, and visions I have recorded on these pages, it seems that I am reading the journal of another man's experiences. Perhaps that is the very nature of humanity; we enter the world in innocence and ignorance, destined to an existence of constant change and growth, hopefully, as a fulfilled and contented person at life's end. I can feel a new man within myself, not sure of his destination, but confident of his path.

The small quarters I am afforded that once seemed cramped now feel like a palace compared to the 14 inches between hammocks where the sailors must take their rest. If I were not dedicated to this quest I have undertaken, I might consider continuing this life at sea. Words cannot convey the exhilaration one feels when the ship is heeled over, the lee rails skimming the water's surface in a stiff, quartering wind, the bow plunging into the green sea, the helmsman leaning into the ship's wheel, keeping the vessel sailing as close to the wind as possible without shivering the sails. The same passion, albeit more tranquil, is also present in the quiet beauty of a sunset on a calm sea, with barely a ripple on its surface.

The only thing of recent note beyond the working of the ship was encountering a convoy of merchantmen on a bearing opposite of our own. At first sighting there was little more than a white spec on the horizon, but shortly numerous sails could be seen breaking into view, with most of the vessels hull-down on the thin line between sea and sky. Before long we beheld scores of ships clustered together close enough to afford them the protection of numbers, but far enough apart to not steal each other's wind. Once determining that we were seeing friendly sails, the captain ordered a change of course to intercept them, in order to get a *report of the weather and sea conditions ahead of us. The captain boarded while we were hove to under the bulk of the massive flagship, trading news of our passages and making purchases of badly needed supplies for the remainder of our voyage.*

It was a surprising and strangely exciting sensation to be amongst people other than the small contingent aboard our vessel. I had not been occupied with feelings of loneliness, perhaps because I have been wholly immersed in my own thoughts, but the brief chance meeting with these mariners filled me with the joy of companionship, with souls of similar experience. I doubt they looked on me as an old salt, but my enthusiasm looked past any patronizing attitudes in our short discourse. Strangers they were, but they felt like brothers, and I saw that same feeling manifested undeniably in their seaman-to-seaman banter across the gap between our two ships.

Our captain returned after a short time, and the crew cast the lines off as we separated slowly to depart, each to our own courses. Final farewells and friendly jibes were exchanged until we fell out of range, and we pulled away from each other; the convoy under clouds of sail, our ship demonstrating its pride with the best show of canvas possible.

Just a few hours later, the reassuring routine of the ship had returned. It's become apparent to me how important rituals of existence are. Men at sea are subjected daily to the harshest environments in the world on a diet that, while plentiful, can hardly be described as beneficial to one's health. Yet they throw themselves into their work with a professional zeal rarely seen in any other occupation. The constant drilling and exercising of their duties assures that they are always prepared for any eventuality and increases the odds of their survival in the worst predicament.

Moreover, they exhibit a tendency to believe in favorable outcomes, possibly because every day is filled with overcoming challenges that become commonplace to them. It is a life they can count on, because they have.

This long cruise has given me the gift of time to contemplate and write about such a variety of subjects that I can scarcely hold it in my mind. I've filled page after page with as much as I can record of the flood of insight that has come to me. It has caused me to look deeply inside my soul, and the introspection has left me fearing that I may not be up to the things I expect to face soon.

What shall I find, what shall I do, and more importantly, who will I become?

. . .

A shadow crosses the pages of his open book, and he looks up from his writing. Looking around, he sees a small bird alight on the rail next to him. The bird looks at him expectantly for a moment, bobbing his head up and down in apparent greeting, skips along the rail, and flies up towards the mainmast. The bird shoots past the lookout, his line of flight pulling the man's attention towards the horizon, as he suddenly call out "Land ho."

William jumps up and leans on the rail, searching in the direction the lookout is pointing towards. He sees a dark shadow on the horizon with cloud cover over it. It's more of a looming presence than a clear view of land, but he trusts that the lookout, 50 feet above the deck on the mainmast, recognizes that they have made landfall. Word is rapidly passed along until moments later the captain appears on the quarterdeck, buttoning his coat, following the lookout's practiced gaze to the horizon. The tone of the ship is transformed, as each expectant eye shifts between the captain and the land, which is now becoming more distinct, awaiting the instructions that will come as surely as the last they received. The captain calmly consults the navigator on their position, his chronometer on the time, and issues the anticipated orders to stand off and wait for the incoming tide. And once again, the routine dutifully returns.

William's Roots

I think I've gone miles beyond the question of, "Is this really happening?" I still can't see what the closing scenes of this story will look like, but I am undeniably being guided on a very specific journey. And I won't even ask the obvious question – "Is this just happening inside my head?" because I think it has a pretty obvious answer, "Doesn't everything happen in there?"

It's starting to feel like a really long road trip (one of my favorite things to do). Whether you've been to your intended destination or not, somewhere along route you start to see the signs telling you in no uncertain terms that you're almost there. And as you get close, it finally starts to feel real, like you're actually, finally going to get there. It's weird how most possibilities don't seem real until you're in the middle of them, maybe because we don't let them inside our head until we want to. Maybe the more accurate assertion would be – it's not real *until* it's inside your head.

William is inside my head, along with every other revelation that brought me to this point. I've seen the signs, so I know I'm close, just like he does.

At the beginning of my story, when I was seeing his name everywhere, I stumbled upon the etymology of it. William is one of the most popular male names of all time. I was not aware of this. It is of Germanic origin and is a compound of two words, "wil" meaning will or desire, and "helm", meaning helmet or protection. So William translates to "the will to protect."

It's no surprise to me that *his* name is William.

I have to admire William. I don't have a clue what the focal point of his quest is, but he has certainly made a heroic commitment to follow through on it. All I've had to do is a little metaphorical time travel to find some answers that apparently have been inside me (and are, therefore, real), all along. By contrast, William has seemingly uprooted his entire life for his journey. If I ever meet him, I will give him a heartfelt and respectful handshake.

As I expected, Steph is thrilled with this latest revelation. I shared it with her over breakfast, and she was full of questions.

"That's what this whole thing has been about, right?" I said, "More and more questions?"

"Sure," she said, "but questions lead to answers!"

Bloody optimist.

"Right, well at least I am getting something now about William. For so long I was getting pulled along in different directions – and I know – I needed to go there to get where I am!" I said quickly, heading her off from the reply she was already forming.

"Do you have any feelings about what's coming next?" she said carefully.

"I don't know," I sighed. "We've had so much happen in our lives, it could be anything," I said, thinking of the loss of my sister, my mom, my stepfather, and the experiences with our kids – there had been so many events that I probably didn't learn from, like I could have and should have.

"Have you thought about Jacob?" she asked.

"Every day since this began," I sighed, "I think it's inevitable, this has all been about the hard lessons – what have we lived through that could be harder? If it's not Jacob, it's really going to be a plot twist."

"And what do you think?"

"I think that, with the way this has happened, I don't feel as scared about it as I did before." I admitted. "Seeing the other side, the missing parts, has made the hard things okay, like now I see them from a different perspective."

We finished our meal in silence, both thinking about how many times that had happened since we were married, promising ourselves not to miss any more parts.

Journal entry – February 20, 2020

When I first picked up my old journals to reread them, I was secretly hoping that I would find secret messages hidden in my entries, which I would magically catch the meaning of. Didn't happen. Looking back, the messages that I got from them did wind up with a magical quality to them, just not in such a sensational way. So I've given up looking for them and focused more on the simple truths I was trying to save as they were revealed to me.

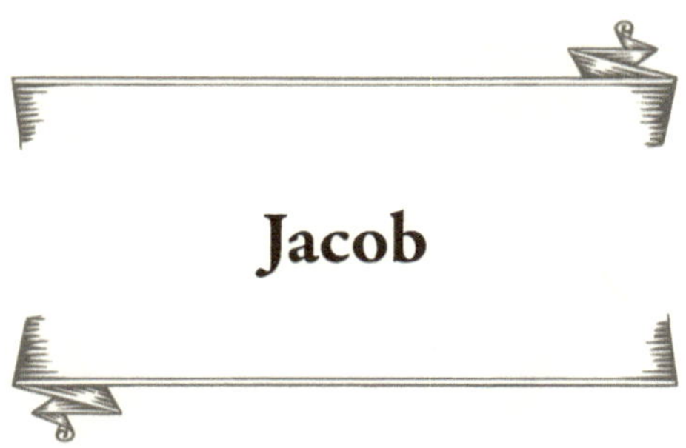

Jacob

Today is moving along with a singular kind of energy; a feeling different than anything I remember feeling in my 60 years of being an earthling. It's like a peaceful walk off a pier. No, that's not right. It doesn't feel wrong or bad, just big, very big – something that regular words aren't fit to describe, because it's not a regular thing I'm heading for. Maybe like David felt on his way to the Giant. Momentous, maybe that's it – a landmark event in my life. Now I'm just being silly. But I do have a sense that something big is coming, because, just like entering that new city for the first time, I've seen the signs.

That still isn't right, but I've decided it doesn't matter if I can find fit words for it. It's there, and I recognize it, and that's enough. I have the peace that comes from knowing. So I went to work, did my thing there, ran a few errands on the way home, fed our dog, Jasmine, had dinner, and eventually sat down to paint a little before bed. I purposely stayed away from horses as subject matter. I made an attempt at a journal entry describing how I felt, but still was not very successful at finding just the right thing to say.

Laying my journal down, I closed my eyes and felt more relaxed than I have probably felt since I was a baby.

. . .

In an instant I'm sitting in the beanbag chair. Ken and Donna are there, as I thought they would be. I loved them at that moment more than I ever knew I could. How could I live so close to them for so long and not be able to explain how much I loved them?

"Thank you both," I said.

My older, and always funky brother just looked up and said, "Sure thing, bro."

Donna was looking at me, serene and tranquil. I swallowed thickly and said, "This is the first time we've been together since you had to leave. I never got to say goodbye. I've missed you, Sis."

She sighed and said, "Of course you miss me. I'm awesome."

"Yes, you are. All those times we were here, before, neither one of you ever said anything." I said, "I didn't think you were really here, I thought you were just part of landscape in my dreams."

"We were both here, and we were both part of your dreams. Don't worry about how it works," She said, seeing my confusion. "There's a lot we can't understand in mortality. It's kind of a butterfly thing; you can't understand what it's like to fly until you've left the cocoon."

"Right, the ox is slow, but the earth is patient – got it."

My beautiful sister smiled and said, "Are you ready?"

"I am."

"We love you."

"I know," I said, "and I love you too."

I sit there for a moment, then stand up and walk to the door. I open it to see myself at work again. I've just taken a call informing me that our three-month-old son, Jacob, has been taken to the ER. It's a busy day at work, so I quickly let people know that I have to leave and run out to my car. I'm driving across town towards the hospital, thinking that I'm overreacting, half laughing at myself for driving too fast to what's most likely going to be something that's not as bad as it sounded.

I run into the waiting area and am quickly escorted directly into the ER, where I find my beautiful wife, collapsing in shock and anguish, and I see Jacob, tiny, laying on a gurney, surrounded by people, whose faces and body language scream that they have done all they could, and it wasn't enough. Their hands are at their sides, there's nothing left to be busy about. Some look at me with deep empathy, some look away, one chastises me for banging on the door in tortured frustration – telling me to settle down.

As I watch, I stand there remembering exactly what I felt like the first time I saw this happen.

It had just become another one of those moments when the whole world stops, but only for us. At first you almost laugh, because the idea is ludicrous. It can't be true, they're just wrong. Nothing anyone says means anything at all. Time isn't even real. It's just noise and light and confusion of thought, and the absolute belief that any second now, you will genuinely explode all over the walls. It's the beginning of more bad days, endless bad days, and more effing questions.

Except it's not. Not this time.

Now, looking at Jacob, so tiny on the emergency room table, all I see is an innocent soul who, like Kate, maybe had nothing to prove by staying here. Lying there completely at peace, he never had to feel the pain inflicted by a cold, indifferent world. The first time I saw him there was so much different; a sight no parent should ever have to behold. I see myself, and Stephanie, surrounded by our families, and I know the things that will come next for us. I don't feel the same anguish. The long passing of years and learning have taken some of the pain away. There have been many questions, but answers have come too. Years of love and learning and trials – some that end with success, others with failure. Too much to see in this moment, but I know them all by heart because we experienced them all, together.

We were a young and happy family when Jacob died. I had recently completed college and was gainfully employed, our daughter was still a toddler, and we were in the middle of building our first home. Every day after work, I rushed home, slammed down dinner, and went to work on the house that I had designed for us. Everything was going as well as a young couple could expect. Both of our families were close by and it seemed like clear skies ahead. We were all healthy, and our biggest decisions involved deciding what to have for dinner, and picking out color schemes and light fixtures for the new house.

Jacob died in the middle of the project. That was when we found out about SIDS, or Sudden Infant Death Syndrome. What a name. SIDS is one of the acronyms given that stand for "Even with our wonderful technology, we have no idea why this happened." Stephanie went looking for real answers – answers that she found, while I spent my endless evenings at our new home, pounding more nails into the walls than any house could ever need. It was many months before we were able to come back to what seemed like a normal life. When that veritable tsunami of emotion hit us, it took a long time for the flood to subside, and it left our whole existence in disarray. Part of our world changing was that it became much, much smaller. I still had a job to go to every day; we still had a house to finish, a beautiful little girl to take care of, and each other. Not much else mattered. Our rescue came in two forms: our daughter Shannon, who was still young enough to need our full attention, the exact blessing we needed to work through our pain – and the spirituality that we found in due course. The hurt never goes way, but it does change. Even after more than 35 years, every so often something reminds me of Jacob, especially the question, "How many kids do you have?" We have four with us, but we have five, and always will.

Of all the questions that came, one had been paramount at the time – why? How could this happen to us? Why now? Why did he have to die? There was no answer to that last and hardest of questions, not in the way we were seeking. But after time and much searching, we did receive an answer – and it was that all along, we had been asking the wrong question. The question that you find you must ask is not why did someone die, it is, why did they live? And that question had, and continues to have, many answers, and they differ from experience to experience, and day to day.

Like the pages in my journal, I can feel each of those individual days – even the missing ones. Our lives are laid out before me, not in the sense of it flashing before my eyes in a bad way, more like a living family album, and I remember every wonderful page. I look down at my hands and see the scars, calluses, and lines of all the years of love and worry and everything else deeply etched into my skin, and each one is a story. I see the beautiful laugh lines around Stephanie's perfect green eyes.

I look up from my hands, and I'm now standing in the golden field again, walking along the same lane. And he's there again – Dad. And my younger self is still walking with him.

I watch myself turn my small head, look back, and smile, and then I realize it's not me. It's Jacob that was, and is walking with him, and his smile to me speaks volumes.

It's the first time I've seen him since I was a young man. It was only nine years after my father passed that Jacob left us. For more than 45 years I've wanted to speak to my father and nearly as long to Jacob. There have been countless things I've wanted, needed to ask them; to tell them both about my worries, my failures and triumphs – but not now. It doesn't occur to me to interrupt them. Jacob's smile says it – this time is for them, ours will come later.

I watch them walk down the lane and only then notice the butterfly flitting along, flying behind them, following them down the lane. Once again – I have found resolution.

. . .

I wake up with a smile and tears on my face. My dream is so perfectly fresh in my mind that I hardly feel like I've left it. I have no thought about trying to hold onto it before it escapes; it isn't necessary, for what I saw is now part of me. To think of forgetting it is laughable, impossible. I don't feel any worry about what comes next. But I write it down anyway.

A New World

Days later I'm still walking around in my own little bubble of tranquility. I'm making sense of things from my past with such clarity that I've even been calm driving in heavy traffic – for real. There are still past events in my life that were never completely resolved, but the missing parts of the stories of Kate, Donna, Jacob, and my dad were enough to bring me to a new place, with a new perspective. It feels like I've reached the end of a journey, my final destination, and there's peace in the realization.

There has been so much to process in my mind that I haven't even been thinking about William as much. He's still in the back of my mind, but I've relaxed my efforts to try to bring myself to him. I've come to the conclusion that we'll meet if and when we're supposed to. This is me, being patient.

I've felt a burden of worry and pain lift, and a new confidence that before I would not have been sure I deserved. But that was me for most of my life. I've always lived under a shadow of doubt and skepticism of my own worth and potential, like I was unexceptional, and had a debt hanging over me that I thought I'd never be able to repay. And I had become too tired to spend the effort.

I now feel like balance has come through some anonymous authority. I don't know how it works, but it feels a lot like my journal – I get more out of it than I put into it. Maybe it's the new perspective working again, and I just need to adjust to it.

Oh, and I've been sleeping like a baby, back to mostly nonsensical dreams that don't hold a commitment over my head. There are no more nighttime monsters, though sometimes I feel like I left William unfinished, inside a closed book, and feel like I should pick it back up so he can move on.

I take that thought to bed with me and lay my head back on the pillow for another peaceful night.

. . .

I'm drifting in clouds of color, sinking through warm water, finally spreading and organizing into a landscape below me that I come to rest on. I've returned to the barn, to a perfectly still and quiet moment. I walk around and can't find Edgar, Bob, or anyone else. Walking over to the flowing, painted field, I find it empty, as well; I feel like I am the only thing moving. It's completely silent but there is still a buzz of energy present, an expectancy that something is about to happen.

In the distance I hear a bell faintly calling to me through a stand of trees, so I begin to walk towards it. I pass through the trees, into the large field full of tall, golden sea grass overlooking a harbor, with a ship just dropping anchor and furling its sails. The fluid, painted colors of the landscape come to rest and resolve themselves into reality. I know it's there without looking, but I turn anyway, to see the house on the hillside to my right – the house with the book.

I hear the bell ringing again, ding-ding, ding-ding; four bells in the afternoon watch, 2:00 pm. My view shifts to the ship, and I see William on deck, sitting on a chair and writing again. Walking around him, I see that he is making a hurried journal entry. It feels a little voyeuristic to read over his shoulder, but I feel like I'm supposed to see it, or at least that I really, really want to.

. . .

William

Day 60 – We have been standing offshore for several interminable days, awaiting favorable wind and tide, which we were fortunate to receive today. With nature's blessing, we are finally making slow headway up the channel that has tantalized us for days. Before long we should see our destination, the sheltered harbor at the channel's end. The vessel's motion has calmed since we fell under the protection of the land, and we are now gliding in with a steady following sea. The crew that are not engaged in working the ship populate the rails and rigging, craning for a glimpse of the next port-of-call.

Closing my journal, I walk over to the few vacant feet of space left along the ship's rail, so I can take in our first view of land in two months' time, and capture in my memory this moment that I have been so anxiously awaiting. Having cleared the neck of the bay, we can now see the port. It is bustling with activity, with dozens of bumboats and launches plying back and forth between the ships at anchor and the quays that line the contours of the busy harbor.

The captain gives orders that send the crew into a flurry of activity: backing the sails to slow the vessel, dropping anchor, and swinging the ship into the wind and tide. Further orders have one group of men furling the sails, another preparing the cargo to be off-loaded, and passengers to disembark. As the ship finishes its swing on the mooring cable, the hillside overlooking the port comes into view.

I can see the house, exactly as I saw it in my dreams.

As soon as I have the opportunity, I make my farewells to my shipmates and give my compliments to the officers, particularly to the captain, who I have come to know and respect. He is one of the few souls with whom I have shared the peculiar nature of my spiritual journey. He has offered me many insights, and much wisdom that he has gleaned from his years at sea, some metaphorical, but many more plain truths that I find creditable. I suppose one cannot live within the bounds of God's most enormous and powerful creation without finding some wisdom in its mysteries. One of the truths I learned by my own observations was that even with the singular importance of the harmonious efforts of the crew to the collective life of the ship, each individual soul onboard is ultimately responsible for his own preservation, both physical and by extension, spiritual. His parting counsel to me is to keep my faith, and remember that a smooth sea never made a skillful sailor.

We say our goodbyes, and I gather my belongings and walk down the gangway, taking a few last moments to look back at my temporary home. As the last passengers disembark, others are already queuing up by the ship, looking fresh and eager. I think of them less as strangers as I would have before, and more as kindred spirits, and I acknowledge that they are preparing to begin journeys of their own, every bit as important to them as mine are to me.

It feels strange to have finally arrived at my destination, even stranger to be on solid ground. I stumble as my feet fall unsteadily on the lifeless brick flagstones on the quay, anticipating the living movement of the decks that does not come. My land legs begin to come back to me, as I pass through the dockyard and shops and make my way towards the house on the hill.

I pause a moment to take in the sights and sounds that seem foreign after so long at sea. Even more powerful are the intoxicating fragrances that are so much more varied than the salt air, tarred rigging, and rank mixture of the lower decks, that have been my entire world. The scent of greenery wafting in on the inland breeze, the pleasant aromas of the bakery and harbor cafés and shops, and the occasional perfume from patches of flowers, all mingle to make a heady blend that overwhelms my senses. How can it feel so new? One would think I had never smelled a new blossom.

The sun is lowering in the sky, blanketing the entire vista with a glowing, golden hue. In the middle of it all, the house is agreeably situated in a glowing field of flaxen sea grass, crossed with a tranquil path.

. . .

I'm standing in the field again and William is in front of me, walking up the path. What can you possibly say to someone who crossed time to find you?

I feel strange, apprehensive, not sure how to begin. I blurt out, "William?" I can already tell what he's going to say.

"Yes, do you know me?"

"No, I don't, but I've seen you."

"Yes, I have been seeing you, as well."

"In dreams." I say as a statement, not a question.

"Yes, in dreams," he said.

"My name is...Robert." I couldn't let him think he came all this way across time and tide, to meet a guy named Bob. "I've been looking for you for a long time. Can you tell me why you've come here?"

"Why, to find you of course. You brought me here."

I sighed and said. "I was thinking that you brought me here. Are you sure your name isn't Edgar?"

He looked at me, confused, and said emphatically, "I assure you, my name is William."

"I'm sorry, I just thought that my whole purpose in finding you was to find answers, and once again, I just have more questions."

"As do I," he replied.

"Are you real, or are you another part of my dream?" I asked.

"I could ask you the same question, sir."

"I'm real, but I'm not sure this all is," I said, looking at the scene around us.

"It seems that we are both in a similar situation," he said. "I began having what I must call visions of you some time ago. I saw you in the house and I sensed you were in some terrible turmoil, and that somehow we had a great connection, at least in purpose, and perhaps in our destinies."

"Which is exactly why I felt I needed to find you. And you came all this way, left everything behind you to find me?"

"I told you, it was a great connection," he said.

"Did you leave your family to come here?"

Haltingly he said, "I had no family left to leave."

"I was afraid of that, I could tell you were going through a very difficult time." I said. "May I ask what happened to your family?"

"There was a great illness passing through the land, my wife and children all succumbed to it. I alone was spared."

I searched his face and saw the depths of his suffering, as well as the healing and the strength of character that it gave him.

"You have to be a man of powerful conviction," I said, "to have made such a journey."

"I am a man. I do not know how I measure up compared to the strength of others, but I know that I must do what I believe to be right," he said. "But the question I came here to ask you still remains. What is it that I can do for you?"

Pausing, I said, "I think you've already done it, William." My quest happened here, while I was searching for you. I think I had to bring a finish to some of the stories in my life before I could be led to yours. The journey I took to find you was exactly what I needed to find the healing that I couldn't have found otherwise. I suppose you were the goal I needed to set my sights on to find the strength to make the journey."

"So we find ourselves knowing that the purpose of our coming together was simply for each of us to have a reason to make the journey."

"They always say it's the journey, not the destination," I said, smiling. "My journey was spiritual. It makes me feel incredibly selfish to be the reason for you to come all this way for the benefit of a perfect stranger."

It was now his turn to study me. "Robert," he began quietly, "I cannot question the power of the inspiration I felt as I considered where my path lay. For these many years since I lost my family, I have been a man without purpose. Before my sea journey began, I had been long on a different one, trying to find what was meant for the years that still lie ahead of me," He said. "Stranger or no, if my coming here has been of service to you, it may be that it was what was meant to happen, and for that, my reward may be that you brought me to a place where I may find the purpose for the rest of my life."

"I have a suspicion it's the same for both of us." I said. "I don't know what else to say except to wish you the joy of finding that purpose. I hope I can live up to the debt of what this has cost you."

"But it is the cost that determines the value, sir," he said. "If I had not spent my effort, I would not have the reward."

"I see that now, but this is not what I expected to happen, and I have no idea where we go from here."

"And that, Robert, is the very description of a most grand and gratifying adventure!" He smiled. "It may be that one day we will both see more of each other that we cannot see now."

"From a different perspective."

"Yes, this may just be the first chapter in our story," he said.

"What will you do now?"

"As I came from the East, I feel I must continue to go west." He said in a matter-of-fact way.

"Is it so easy to decide?" I asked.

"I must go forward or back," he replied.

"Before you leave, could we walk for a while?" I asked.

"I should like nothing better," he said with a smile.

As we began walking down the lane, I looked at William and thought, "It's a whole new world."

Buried Treasure

It's been months since my adventure with William came to its conclusion. We entered each other's lives suddenly and unexpectedly, for a very specific purpose. Simply put, we each lacked the roadmap to take our lives in directions we needed to go, and taking on the mission of helping someone else charted those courses for us both. Such a simple and precious concept that we all too often fail to grasp – that we usually try harder to make changes in our lives for the benefit of others, more readily than do it for ourselves. It is the wisdom and richness of friendship and family – they make us want to be better.

I still think about William frequently, even though I never did find out exactly who he was or where he had come from – or where he wound up for that matter, but I got a strong impression that he had ben succeeded in finding the purpose he had been searching for. Although brief, our friendship was born of shared life-changing experiences that served to set our paths in motion, and like I found my answers, I knew he would have found his. A man with such courage and conviction cannot be held back from finding his purpose. I searched for him for a while on the slim chance that I could find a stranger from 200 years ago by just their first name. Even with the power of the Interwebs, I knew that "slim" was a colossal understatement. As an extra measure, I even paid a visit to a local pet store and brought a bird home with me (I named him Bob). Bob hangs out with me on his perch in my home office, and yes, he's a bit of a smart aleck. Over time I remembered less often to look for William, and eventually I shifted back to my own family's genealogy work.

Recently I ran into a wall with my latest family history research, so I was doing web searches to try to confirm the identity of a lost ancestor. In the process of trying to locate him I was investigating our old family homestead history and stumbled upon some interesting information.

On the family tree that my uncle published for the family in 1973, there is a simple hand-drawn map showing the Thompson family homestead's location in the vicinity of Atwell's crossing in Butler County, near Annandale, PA. This region of western Pennsylvania sits within a few miles of the Ohio state line and is a rich hardwood forest. Much still remains the same in the wooded area around the old homestead; however, I was viewing the region with Google Earth and noticed a large parking lot and a road almost directly over the original homestead site. The thing that caught my eye was that while the lot and road were paved, the road only went a short distance and then ended at what looked like a tunnel entrance. Referring back to the old map, I saw something I hadn't previously noticed – an old limestone mine. Now I was seriously intrigued, so I did another quick search and found that our old family homestead is now the location of Butler County's Iron Mountain, a huge underground data storage facility built in the old mine. 220 feet beneath the surface, the mine is now home to more than 200 acres of high-tech, super-secure data storage for the U.S. government and some of the largest American corporations, in a six-by-three-mile block. Along with the server storage facility, the giant underground bunker also holds some of our nation's most prized artifacts and important records, such as original recordings of Frank Sinatra, photos of Marilyn Monroe, and other historical icons, and, the remains of Flight 93, from the al-Qaeda attacks on the U.S.

It is a fascinating fun fact to find, and yet when I return to my original train of thought, the information I'm seeking is much more important to me than the innumerable petabytes of data buried in the ground, below our old family garden plot.

Returning to my initial search I started scrolling deeper through the results (looking harder), and I saw a number of black and white images that had the appearance of historical photos, and I began looking through them to see if I would find any other jewels of information. I love historical photos because they often hold so much emotion in them. Photography served a different purpose in that era. It was a time well before selfies and other such vain things. It was the beginning of a new art form, and was reserved for storytelling on a much more significant scale. One of the old, faded images I found showed a farmer with his young family, posing by a plow horse. According to the story, the man operated a farm in, oddly enough, the exact location of our family's homestead. The sight of the man's face in the photo hit me like a thunderbolt – with shaking hands I nervously clicked on it to see an enlarged view, and saw the very familiar face of a young, contented man smiling at the camera – obviously a man who had happily, finally, found his purpose. And I had found mine.

At the bottom of the faded, curled print was an inked-in caption – "William Thompson, farmer – circa 1758."

Two Chairs and a Pen

The window in our bedroom is open, and the lace curtains are fluttering gently. The morning light is sending dancing shadows around the room. It feels like I'm back on the ship, with the rippling patterns of light on the cabin walls that had reflected off the water through the ship's portholes. I can almost smell the salt air.

This is one of those mornings when a good long stretch convinces me that I'm not going anywhere; I'm just too comfortable not to relish it. This moment is too good to waste, so I grab some of the ten extra pillows on the bed and prop them up behind me. When I arrange them to absolute perfection I lay back and look up to see a small table...with the book on it, and I really do smell salt air.

I'm not in our bedroom at home, I'm back in the room overlooking the harbor, but the room has changed. For one thing it has now become more of a bedroom, and there are two chairs by the table with the book. Stephanie is here with me, still asleep in bed. Springing out of bed, I see that this time, the book is open to a blank page. I don't know what this means, but oh boy, I think this is going to be good!

I start at the first blank page and flip through the following ones, and they are also blank. I keep turning the pages to what should be the very end, but no matter how many pages I turn over, there is always another one after it. I quickly go back to the page before the first blank one, and I see my own, last, personal-journal entry. As I keep turning pages towards the front of the book, they also contain my writings, as they appear in my own, real-world journal, except they keep going further back, and there are no missing pages; every day is accounted for. No matter how many pages I flip toward the front, it continues, past the day I first started keeping a journal, past the date of my birth, the pages keep going. The journal is infinite – my whole existence, ready and waiting to flash before my eyes.

I have some reading to do.

I close the journal and look at the cover – my name is engraved on the lower right corner of the cover. It allows me look at it for a moment, then it purposefully opens itself back up to the first blank page, and then I notice the quill pen and ink well sitting next to it.

I'm guessing this is my new pen.

Stephanie is still sleeping, the sun is just coming up, the world is once again bathed in golden light, and it really is a brand new day.

And I still have so much to learn.

The End.

About the Author

Just an artist contentedly living in Alaska since 1967. Married to the bravest person I know.

Read more at www.ArtofAlaska.com.